A Wild Beast at Heart

Rodrigo T. Meirelles

PublishAmerica
Baltimore

First printing

ISBN: 1-4241-4721-2
PUBLISHED BY PUBLISHAMERICA, LLLP
www.publishamerica.com
Baltimore

Printed in the United States of America

Dedication

This book is dedicated to the most important people in the world, my wife, Maria José, my cornerstone and safe haven, and our children, Maria Eduarda and Daniel, the lights of our lives.

Acknowledgments

Many people had a degree of influence in the coming of this book, in one form or another sharing with me a part of their lives, and I am happy I can call them friends. Unhappily, I will never be able to share this achievement with some of them.

I would like to thank Bob Bilton, Frans Bussiahn, John Coningham Netto, George Daniels, Sandor Hauser, Randy Kroeg, Mike Vander Meulen, René Schrauwers, Bob Scott Jr., and especially:

Antônio Roberto Junqueira Meirelles—for his love, ethics, and values
José Haroldo Camargo—for his stability
Antônio Maximiano Tréz Filho—for his *joie de vivre*
João Alfredo Tardelli (*in memoriam*)—for feeding my dreams
Antônio Carlos Silva Valentim (*in memoriam*)—for being my friend

Table of Contents

Foreword

I always enjoyed stories, either as a listener or as a teller, particularly if I was one of the characters, but this is not the reason that I wrote this book.

Everything started with a one-page thank you note to a friend which I tried to get publish, without success, in the form of a very short column. Then, I went hunting on a magic, misty morning and knew I had to share the communion with nature and traveling in space and time with other people and show that there are no limits for our dreams.

My father has been telling us and everybody else that he will one day write a book, *Contos Rurais*. I even gave him pen and paper but have not yet seen a word. Although unwillingly I may have stolen some of his stories.

The decision to finally write a book came on a sad Sunday morning when I was in a train from Amsterdam to Hannover, staring at the wintry fields between the Netherlands and Germany and mourning over the death of a most dear friend, *Chileno*. I felt that even if my train was about to reach the "bend of the world," I would like to leave at least one story behind.

Conceived in the Netherlands, this book was lived and written in bits and pieces, in Michigan (USA), in the Winterberg range (Republic of South Africa), in several farms in Brazil—Taboa (my real birth place), Buriti do Retiro, São Jorge Preto, Ronda—and other places around this "*mundo velho sem porteira.*" I revised it in Shanghai (China) and wrote its final words on my home's deck, on a most beautiful spring afternoon.

Even if you do not enjoy the thrill of the chase and the hunting of game, I hope that you enjoy these stories, and I urge you to hunt your dreams.

Mattawan, May 2006

Why I Hunt

There is no sweeter fragrance than the inebriant essence of a fired shotgun shell, and that same aroma transports me in time and space to my earliest memories, following my father's steps hunting upland birds over our pointing dog, Diana, and retrieving the spent, 28 gauge, paper hulls.

Diana, the English pointer, accidentally died when I was still very young but Diana, the goddess of hunting, has had me under her spell for as long as I can remember. The need to hunt and the pleasure of the chase burn inside me. I live to hunt.

Over the years, I have tried to answer the question of why I hunt using rational and scientific argumentation, talking about the negative impact of human development over nature, the virtual elimination of predators and other animals that compete with society's scarce and disputed economic resources, and rationalizing that the only way to preserve a piece of nature or a little bit of wilderness is by extracting an "economic surplus" from them. Only hunters, among all members of society, are willing to allocate the time and money to manage nature in such way.

However, as I began to dedicate more time to hunting and the outdoors, I also tried to explore not only why I loved to hunt, but why I had to hunt. Which compulsion would make me crave for autumn and winter and dislike summers or how could I explain to my wife that I am not trying to punish myself when I wake up long before first light and go out in inclement weather to hunt? Or worse yet, why I spend more money on my Labrador retriever than on our children's college fund?

After chasing it for many years, from when I hunted quail and shot fish in my childhood in Brazil to going on safari in Africa, I believe I finally found the answer to such pressing and profound questions. It is still rational and scientific, but biological and philosophical instead of economical in its content.

I am not an anthropologist or a philosopher to write a treaty on human evolution or meditate on hunting, I am a hunter, and, as a hunter, I can say that deep in my genes and in my soul, the predator lays, patiently waiting for opportunities to surface and strike upon its prey. I hunt because I am a predator. I am on the top of the food chain and, as part of nature, I must perform my ecological function, occupy my niche, and feed on my prey.

Although detractors of hunting would like us to believe otherwise, *Homo sapiens* are as integral and important components of nature as any other creatures, and as we went through a similar evolution process as all those living creatures, we evolved as the most successful predator this planet has ever had. Evolution shaped us not only physically, but also emotionally and psychologically, and not even in our modern yet stupid time will misguided and ill-intentioned people be able to negate that.

Of course, it could be argued that humans, being rational creatures, should be able to control their most basic instincts, but by doing so, we would only further remove ourselves from the natural world and then nature would play a constantly diminishing part of our life until, by being ignored for so long, it would be forgotten. And if nature becomes unimportant by being ignored and forgotten, what can we expect that will become of it, a wasteland of shopping malls, golf courses and subdivisions or, worse yet, a dump yard for human rejects?

By castrating our instincts and not hunting, we would not only deny ourselves the much needed vacation from our demanding lives and pressing (and some times depressing) routine, the human condition as mentioned by Ortega Y Gasset, vacations in which man can develop true happiness but also risk developing a total disregard for nature, a disregard that could have a most terrible outcomes, the end of all wilderness within human reach.

Hunters, more than any other group in human society, are responsible for conservation since we not only want to be able to hunt today, but also in the future. We want our children and their children to be able to have as close a communion with nature as we do. Hunters have a symbiotic relation with their prey. While hunting provides us nourishment for body and soul, we make our prey stronger by helping providing suitable habitat and maintaining the prey population within the habitat's carrying capacity. Hunters interact with their prey year after year after year.

Because of this constant interaction between hunter and hunted, predator and prey, at one time, I was afraid that the burning ember that keeps the predator alive deep inside us could be extinguished, either by lack of fuel, or by too much fuel, but I no longer worry about that. Due to circumstances of life, I had to spend many years without hunting. It was hard, but I endured and Hemingway, Ruark, and other close friends kept the ember burning. On the other extreme, I was exposed to Africa and not even its abundance of game could tame the predator inside me, for all the excitement of the chase was present again on the first opportunity, either shooting a pheasant over my dog or drawing my bow at a whitetail doe.

The excitement and thrill of the chase, the fulfillment that it gives us, reminds me that men are entitled basic rights, among them *the pursuit of happiness*. But happiness is a state of mind, is doing what we like, pursuing what gives us pleasure. Happiness is in the action, not necessarily in the achievement. Ortega Y Gasset really captured the essence of men's pursuit of happiness in saying, "The hunter does not hunt in order to kill; on the contrary, he kills in order to have hunted."

Since happiness is found in the action, and the continuation of that action, not necessarily in the achievement, then, I hunt not only because I am a predator, but I hunt in order to be happy.

Opening Day

This story was the beginning of this book. My intention was to write a thank you note to my friend Bob Scott for helping me to bag my first deer. The text you now read is an expanded version of the original one page note.

To tell someone in Michigan that I bagged my first deer at age 34 would probably elicit the question: "Where were you in the previous 20 years or so?" Well, I was not in Michigan or even close to it. Since it is not sufficient to say that I hunted before, and that I am a hunter, or at least, I am a hunter in my heart, I must make a short story long and take you around the world with me.

I was raised in a farm in Brazil, "Fazenda Taboa," located deep in the rich red soil of northern São Paulo state—the "Alta Mogiana" region. Just like Scarlet O'Hara got her strength from Tara, I replenish my heart and soul when surrounded by family and friends in the cool veranda or shooting white-winged doves that come to nest on the old mango and giant fig trees, in the few precious days I can visit Taboa each year.

When I was a child, we knew about four deer species in Brazil, from the Labrador-size "veado-mateiro" to the majestic "cervo-do-pantanal," probably bigger than a mule-deer, and one of the largest mammals in South America. Nowadays, biologists tell us there are eight deer species in Brazil, including one identified so recently that the poor animal only has a scientific name and the white-tailed deer, known as Cariacu in Brazil and found in the savannahs of Roraima, north of the Amazon river.

My first contact with deer came when I was four or five years old. My father was driving my mother's car, fast as usual, in the dirt roads we relied on, when we hit a doe of the small (under 60 pounds) "veado-catingueiro" (deer collision is not a privilege of Michigan). While still alive, the little doe could not be saved and her hide was my bedside rug for years.

In Brazil, the traditional way to hunt deer was "ridding the hounds" in a similar fashion to fox hunting in Great Britain, although, I can guarantee I never saw a single hunter with a red coat or even a tie. We enjoy a more relaxed life style in the tropics.

One day, when I was around seven, my father organized such a hunt and invited some friends. It was winter, sometime between June and August when the days are not too hot, the nights are cool and it is very dry. The expedition consisted of about ten hunters and an equal number of horses, twice as many dogs, my mother with a large lunch to be served under old shade trees and a wild bunch of children. Sometime between main course and dessert, the dogs found a deer, the hunters mounted and went after the "toque," as we call the sound and general action of dogs pursuing prey—the chase. We children stayed with my mother and the remains of the lunch, spread over the white tablecloth on the ground, and we did not even have time to be bored. Somehow the "toque" changed direction and that deer, followed by twenty frantic dogs, came running right over the dishes while hunters and horses were kind enough to go around us.

Unhappily today, even with twice as many identified species as thirty years ago, any deer hunting (well almost any hunting at all) is outlawed in Brazil and the consequences are that it is very rare to see a deer or other mammals almost anywhere, unless you go far away from civilization. WARNING: Never allow the eco-terrorists to gain a position in this great country. The kind of damage they can do is unbearable for any one of us who loves the outdoors.

Sometime in late 1999, yours truly, wife and children, packed bags (guns were sadly left behind) and moved away from Brazil, and before landing in Michigan's hunting paradise we had a short three year detour in Europe, with residence in the Netherlands (a country full of good memories and loved friends). While I never had the opportunity (or the disposable income) to hunt in Europe, I had enough game dishes (venison included) in excellent restaurants from Finland to Italy, and saw enough deer and elevated hunting blinds (particularly in Germany) to guarantee you that (even at a high price) there is much more hunting in Europe than we can expect from a totally tamed continent that was the epicenter of two world wars. Just as a note, most of the game served in European restaurants comes from hunted animals and I found enough No. 6 shot in well-prepared pheasant and rabbit across several countries to testify to that.

The quest for **my** first deer started in the 2002 season (shortly after relocating from Europe). First, I dozed off when bow hunting (with a bright Hoyt target bow) and the guy in the next tree shot a fat doe. At least I had the opportunity to teach him how to field dress an animal. Then, in late December, I accomplished the difficult task of missing two deer within fifteen minutes of each other with my new muzzle-loader. Somehow, I doubt it was the gun's fault.

Another year had to go by until I could try again, but this time, due to being back to school (I was pursuing an MBA at Michigan State University) I had only one day to hunt during gun season: Opening Day.

Friday, November 14th, 2003: I left work around 2 pm, drove home, got my gear and my Remington 870 shotgun with a brand new Hastings scoped rifled barrel that I had bought several months before and never fired a single shot through it, four boxes of slugs and went as quickly as possible to the Southern Michigan Gun Club shooting range. At 25 yards, I could not even hit the paper. I just started going nuts.

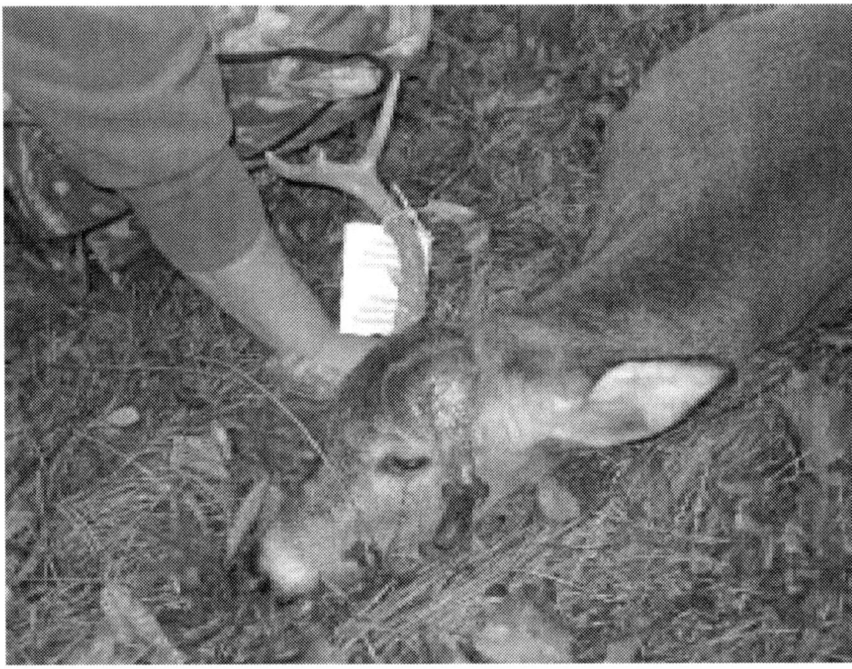

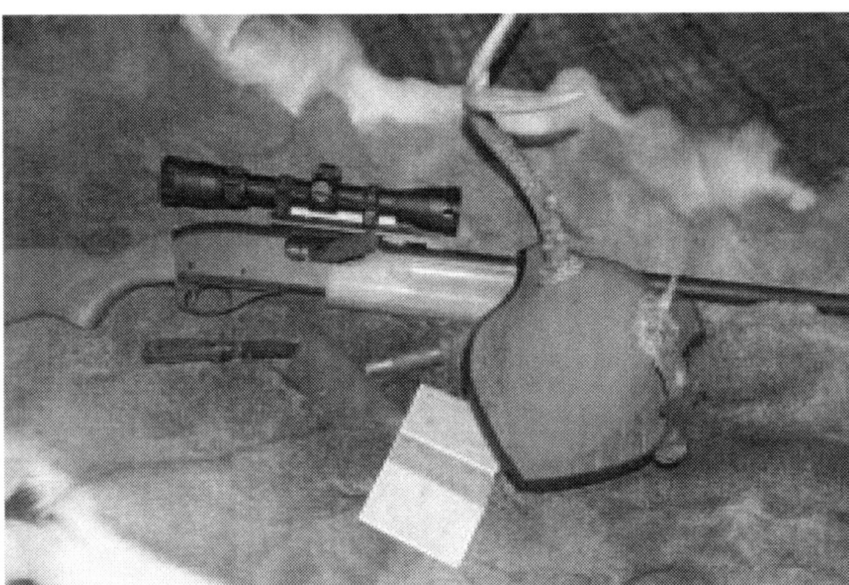

Before despair overtook me, I drove (again, as quickly as possible) to D&R Sporting Center at M-43, just west of Kalamazoo, and had the scope bore sighted in no time by the ever-helpful Bruce. At this time, my confidence was so low that I bought four or five more boxes of slugs to help me in the sight-in. The result was a consistent two inch, three shot group at a hundred yards, just under point of aim.

Saturday, opening day, a long time before first light, I was at my friend Bob Scott's home, met his son who was also aiming for his first deer, prayed that the cold air would disguise the buck fever shrills, packed my ground blind (being much heavier than squirrels, I don't feel comfortable in trees) and the three of us took off to the tree line facing a field that we would hunt. I must say that it takes a lot of a friend to invite you over to opening day when his son is also coming to try for that first whitetail. I can't thank him enough.

By first light, the fusillade almost made me think I was in Iraq or some other part of the world not as nice as Michigan and I started seeing something white across the field, but it was nothing more than some paper taped to a pole. Around eight, I missed, just missed, a very nice buck running at 60 or 70 yards. But since I was quite comfortable in my blind, I endured.

Nature was forgiving to me. About one hour later, a nice sized buck came walking about 40 yards directly in front of me. I took my time, put the cross hairs to his shoulders, kept moving my shotgun like on a very slow "high house" clay pigeon, and could see fur coming out of him when he was hit, and before he took off.

After a quarter of an hour or so, we started trailing him. Bob was the first to find the blood spoor and we located the buck about a hundred yards into the trees (but it felt like a mile after I had to drag him) and for one moment, I felt as if I was robbed of something. The left antler was crooked, twisted downwards and just barely attached to the skull skin. At once, I remembered Robert Ruark's "The Horn of the Hunter" when, after trailing Kudu for several days or weeks, he shoots this prize bull only to find out that he was an immature animal with only one curl in his horns. But this feeling only lasted a moment.

I drove home and brought my family back, so my kids could see that beef (or venison for the matter) doesn't come from "Meijer's" and took the rest of the day butchering and packing the meat. I could say that this story ends at Christmas Eve tasting the very well prepared venison ham, but no. Those unimpressive antlers will keep bringing me back nice memories, especially of friendship. Thank you, Bob.

To know more: Deer species that occur in Brazil

Scientific Name	Popular Name
Blastocerus dichotomus	Cervo-do-pantanal
Mazama americana	Veado-mateiro
Mazama bororo	Veado-bororó
Mazama gouazobira	Veado-catingueiro
Mazama nana	Veado-de-mão-curta
Mazama nemorivaga	
Odocoileus virginianus	Cariacu
Ozotocerus bezzoarticus	Veado-campeiro

The Mists of Michigan

In the fall of 2004 Michigan held its first and, so far, only official dove season in state history. According to the Department of Natural Resources, 4,981 permits were sold and a total of 3,067 hunters actually hunted and killed 28,099 doves.

Ever since relocating from the Netherlands to Michigan in the summer of 2002, I looked forward to the opportunity of hunting mourning doves. Everywhere I read and everybody I spoke to commented on how sportive these birds are, true acrobats of the skies that will bring humiliation even to the most accomplished shotgunners, commanding an impressive ratio of shells fired to birds brought down.

Before and after the 2004 season, the alternative to Michiganders has been to hunt out of state, Indiana being the closest option. Many hunters I know will block their agendas a year ahead and spend September 1st and 2nd in some Indiana farm after the elusive gray bird (I truly believe that a "mourning dove pattern" may be a most effective camouflage for military aircrafts), but both in 2002 and 2003, I could not join the fellow hunters from the Southern Michigan Gun Club, having to travel on work to places as bad as Paris and Honolulu. Such is life.

As fall 2004 approached, I was worried about solving a problem that haunts hunters all over in these modern times: a place to hunt, or the search for a kind soul that not only does not oppose hunting but also does not intend to skin you and your wallet to allow you access to land. Although Michigan has lots of public hunting land, the most convenient locations can be crowded or, in this case, not be dove friendly since they prefer agricultural fields, sorghum and sunflower being top on their list.

But as I am, apparently, a communicative person, my distress was recognized and even non-hunters eventually tried to help. And someone mentioned that Bob Bilton, a colleague at work, planned to hunt doves, and since we had ice fished together before, I reasoned we were friends enough that I could invite myself along.

Bob's wife has an uncle that owns a farm in Watervliet, Berrien County, one of the Michigan counties along the Indiana border elected to hold Michigan's first dove season. One October Sunday morning I drove by Bob's around six (my wife calls that penitence) because neither had any experience on hunting doves and no idea on what time they would start flying nor for how long they would be around and we wanted to be in a field before the start of legal shooting hours. We only had a small problem, finding the field we would hunt because of the thick fog that marked that fall.

We found the field and parked along the tree line that surrounded it, some five hundred yards from the road, gathered our gear and walked back towards the vineyard that stood almost in the center of the cornfield. It was still dark, damp and quite cool. Due to the dove's keen eyesight, we decided to sit inside the vineyard and use the grapes as a natural hunting blind. This was a perfect arrangement. We each had a field of fire of at least 270 degrees with complete safety and, as a further guarantee, we were sure at all times of each other's location.

Once I sat at my chosen place, I started to feel that that day and place were a magical occasion. Due to the mist, I could not see far, but as the first morning lights started to tear the grey veil that enveloped south Michigan, I discovered the small, velvet-black, ripe grapes and to my enormous surprise they tasted just like *jabuticabas*, a typically Brazilian fruit that sounds like "ploft-pluft-nhoc," when bitten. The *jabuticabeira* (*Myrciaria trunciflora*) is a tree that, besides the delicious fruits, was prized by children and adult alike as the source of the highest quality forks around, with which the best slingshots are made. Slingshots were a common hunting tool that children used to pursue *rolinhas* (*Columbina sp.*) and *margozinhas* (*Columba plumbea*), Brazilian doves that remind me of the mourning doves.

Dawn fascinated me so much that I knew I had to write about traveling in time and space on the flavor of an unlikely *jabuticaba* from Michigan.

And then I was brought back to reality, a single dove came overhead and disappeared in front of my eyes, in the mists of Michigan, before I could move my small, 28 gauge Beretta over-under. I confess that I was taught that if the doves would be that fast all day long, I had better chance to bring birds home in the skeet field (but skeet field birds probably would make poor table fare). As the day grew lighter, doves started flying over us from all the points of the compass, in ones and twos and tens. It was just an amazing air raid.

The little mourning dove is a deceivingly fast flier and it took me a good many shots to start connecting the pattern of my 28 to the maneuvers of the doves. Shooting was fast and furious but we would always attempt to retrieve the birds as soon as we hit them because they are very difficult to find in the harvested corn field. Their color blending perfectly to the straw and the ground, and neither of us had a dog (but I am working on that as I write). Then, when the doves were swarming the skies, an incident happened: Bob ran out of shells. Tragedy.

At the peak of bird activity on years past and to come, we had to drive looking for a store that had 20 gauge ammunition. We found plenty at Meijers.

The round trip took us about an hour and when we came back,

enough birds were around but nothing like before and we decided to take a small break—hard salami, some cheese, water and search for downed birds. We hunted for about another hour and decided to go home, taking a lot of empty shells and seven delicate birds.

Bob refused to keep any birds saying that there was not enough of them for two and asked me to take them home, but that was not really proper, so we came to good terms. I took the birds home, my wife prepared them in a beautiful and delicious dish with green beans and bacon based on a German hunting book she gave me once for Christmas when we lived in the Netherlands and Bob and I savored it in, of all places, our office restaurant to the amazed looks of several co-workers. Due to corporate regulations, we could not enjoy a good bottle of Rioja but hopefully there will always be the coming season.

Dove Breasts with Bean Salad

Breasts of seven doves (more for more people or better shots)
Savory
1 ½ pounds green beans
Half an onion
Vinegar, salt, olive oil, mustard
½ pound cherry tomatoes (if you like tomatoes, I don't)
¼ pound breakfast bacon
Butter

Boil the savory in salted water for five minutes, then remove. Clean the beans, blanch in the same water so that they are still crisp, leave to drain and place in a dish.

Chop the onion and sprinkle over the beans. Make a vinaigrette from four table spoons vinegar, a little mustard, and eight table spoons olive oil. Pour the vinaigrette over the beans. Quarter the tomatoes and add to the beans (not if I am eating this dish). Cut the bacon into strips, pan-fry, and sprinkle over the salad.

Brown the pigeon breasts in the butter, season with salt (I don't like pepper), cover and simmer until cooked. Lay the breasts on the beans. Serve this light dish with fresh white bread, and with a good red wine (tonight I would pick *Condessa de Leganza*)

21 Feet of Muscles

The first house I remember living in was the farm house of *Santa Genoveva*, then part of our family property which was divided by the *Córrego do Rosário*, a dark water stream that was the centerpiece of much of my early contact with fishing and hunting.

This house represented the typical, practical, northern São Paulo state architecture designs of the 1940s and 1950s when coffee was still king. Brick and mortar, ceramic tiles and shingles, large windows, high ceiling and spacious rooms that make the house fresh and cool even in the warmest summer days.

In a small guest room that connected the front door, which opened to a large patio and then a larger garden, and the dining room, there was a cabinet of 1960s vintage with slim long legs, two or three drawers and two sliding glass doors. The cabinet could be slightly different from this but memory plays strange tricks on us. Along with normal glassware and the odd bottle of Ballantine's Scotch whisky, that cabinet guarded some treasures: samples of sorghum seeds, an agronomist magnifying glass, the case of a Cougar hunting knife, and two old photos of uncertain age.

Those yellowish and wrinkled black and white photos, one of them partially torn, showed two *sucuris* (*Eunectes notaeus*) or anacondas killed at my great-grandfather's farm, laying across a street in Morro Agudo, a nearby town, the longer of the two stretching from a sidewalk to the other. The second snake was four or five feet less and much slimmer. While, at the time, I never had the curiosity to measure the width of the streets in Morro Agudo, people around our house would tell me that the largest of the snakes was at least 10 meters (30 feet) long, and perhaps stretched as much as 12 meters (36 feet) and that it was the largest snake ever seen around our part of the country.

When I came to school age, we moved to town. The photos remained at the left cabinet drawer at the Santa Genoveva house and stories continued to be told; sucuris that swallowed whole deer and were found only with the antlers outside their mouths, babies that disappeared when their mothers went to wash clothes on the rivers and many more. Almost every time we would go to the farm, I would look at those photos, stare at the sucuris and return them to their resting place (today, almost 30 years later, I wish I still had those photos).

Then, one weekend during the Brazilian winter of 1980 (I had to ask my mother for the year and Brazilian winters are from June to August), I finally saw, live and in color, the largest snake I ever came across. We were on our way to a polo game (something I was never particularly fond of) at the *Fazenda São Judas*, and since we had to drive by our farm to get there, we stopped at it so my father could take care of some business. As we were about to leave, the group of people that were coming to fish just downstream from our old powerhouse started calling for help because of a huge snake that was laying on the grass.

My father and others ran down to the stream and saw the very big sucuri (I just can't use the word "anaconda"; it does not sound proper to me). My father asked the others to help him capture the snake because he wanted to send it to a zoo due to its enormous size, and five or six men quickly joined him in trying to pull that snake away from the river, but the sucuri had a different opinion and did not quite agree with my father's noble goals.

By the time they could get a hold of the serpent, it had its head and part of its body in the water and "had a hold" of something, and, no matter how hard the men tried, they could not move that snake a single inch.

Now, a sucuri is a very powerful animal, a non-poisonous snake that feeds on alligators and mammals as large as deer and capybara (or calves and pigs if they are handy) and kills their prey by constriction. The sucuri, after securing the prey with its jaws, wraps itself around the animal and literally squeezes it to death. If nothing else, the result is a reptile with muscles that would cause envy to a bodybuilder.

Another characteristic of snakes is that the skin is cold and smooth and when in a humid environment, it feels like it is lubricated. Without any place to grip, fighting that snake must be like trying to pull on an oiled crowbar.

Since, after much pulling and stretching, no progress was being achieved, my father decided to try to grab the serpent by its head and untangle it from whatever underwater hook it was holding to. Because of the steep river bank, he had to come to his knees and support his body with his left arm while he moved the right hand along the snake's body searching for its neck (or what would be a neck on a snake). Just as he was doing this, the head of the sucuri came out of the water and it grabbed my father's left hand.

Mr. Candinho, a long time farm employee and one of my father's hunting partners, was standing guard from the beginning of the fight and as the sucuri grabbed my father's hand he shoved the barrel of the 12 gauge shotgun against the snake and fired and since it did not let go, he reloaded and fired again, this time almost separating the serpent's head from its body.

During all the commotion, my mother had kept all her precious children away from danger, up the bank and across the fence on the road, but now, with the great animal dead, but still contracting its muscles, every one, including less brave people that were too busy to help before, wanted a piece of the action. And all help was welcome to load that monster in the back of my father's Chevrolet pick-up.

After everyone present had the opportunity to touch the cold reptile skin, we continued to our planned destination, the polo game, and the now dead and apparently warmer sucuri invited a lot of curiosity, a lengthy photo section and some more stories about longer and larger snakes or more dangerous situations depending on who was the storyteller.

Later that night, the sucuri was skinned, the fat carefully saved as it can be used to heal rheumatisms and some skin infections and over two hundred pounds of meat were divided among farm employees and friends in town.

Even before you ask I must say, yes, sucuri tastes just like chicken (or perhaps catfish).

We measured that sucuri at just over seven meters long, or around twenty one feet but as the number seven in Brazil is associated with, totally unheard of, fishermen and hunters' lies, when the hide came back from the tannery, it measured just over six meters or eighteen feet because a part of it was cut off during the processing.

We still have that skin at my parent's home and it is always a source of amusement for visitors when we display it. We have a picture of our son Daniel wrapped from toes to neck in it.

Unfortunately, the tanning process did not preserve the beautiful contrasting black and brown colors or the elasticity of the scales but it is still possible to admire it and imagine the power of the largest snake in the American continent and one of the largest in the world.

The Winterberg Journal

The Winterberg is the highest mountain in the region of Adelaide, a small city in the Eastern Cape province, Republic of South Africa, being over 2,500 meters high, and it was a constant and trusted companion during my first safari appearing ethereal in the horizon during most of my chases.

Day 1 29 May 2005 (The Beginning)

We got to camp yesterday, via Port Elizabeth, met our professional hunters, Frans, Stuart and Edward (Ed), sighted our rifles, discussed expectations and desires over dinner. Today, I had my first day on safari, hunting Africa.

We started the day hunting kudu, a magical animal, the grey ghost, which eluded Hemingway and Ruark. We climbed my first hill in Africa, got to a vantage point and glassed the opposing hills. We saw many kudu cows and young males but no shooters or trophies. Afterwards, we stalked a big impala ram that was most uncooperative by not presenting itself to be shot.

At this time, I realized that whatever you wish to hunt or shoot in

Africa is up a hill, out there, and not exactly on the same hill you are. I climbed more steep slopes in one morning in Africa than in probably most of my life (but I must say that I lived in reasonably flat ground most of the time).

In between the not-shot impala and lunch, we came across a small springbok herd and around 11:15 AM, I shot my first African game animal, a nice, black springbok ram with 11 and 3/8 inch horns. One shot kill at about 160 meters while standing inside an acacia thorn bush (all PHs we worked with had laser rangefinders, so the distances are quite accurate and not wild guesses).

After lunch and a nap (or siesta), we went back to kudu or bushbuck. This was a most exciting afternoon.

As we parked the truck and started trekking to our vantage point (again, uphill), a warthog dashed away from some undergrowth. Some minutes later, a noise came out of the bush and, suddenly, a kudu cow came jumping out and fell right on top of some acacia thorns. Every reasonable person knows that she was not charging but the anticipation is what really counts. Adrenalin rushed up and I had my rifle trailing that cow just as I would do with a "low house" clay pigeon on station 5 in a skeet field.

As we continued trailing, uphill, Mongezi, our tracker, spotted a bushbuck, one of Africa's most beautiful antelopes. We scouted this particular animal for almost two hours before I could take a shot. Up and down hill, closer and farther, the sun shining on my rifle barrel and turning my scope in a perverse flashlight. We lost him in the bush until a young kudu bull spooked by Frans made him move again.

I shot my bushbuck at about 170 meters (or yards, who cares?) and he went down out of sight. As the light was starting to fade, Frans asked me to go along with Mongezi while he covered the general area with his rifle in case the animal tried to escape while we approached him. Frans was kind enough to remind me that bushbucks are very dangerous animals that will often charge when wounded.

Again, the approach was very exciting but we had to climb down a hill and climb up another before we reached the area the animal was when shot. We found the animal, dead from a fatal, if somewhat misplaced, neck shot. And disaster struck me once more. This absolute huge bushbuck, 15 and 1/4 inches horn length, suitable to ingress in the prestigious Rowland Awards big game record book, had a single horn, the missing one broken at the base.

My heart and soul are twisting at this moment. What to do with this magnificent animal? I need to think.

Day 2 30 May 2005 (Climbing in life)

Today, I had one of the most demanding hiking and climbing actions of my life. Early in the morning, we started for kudu and, as it must always be the case in Africa, the animals we wanted were up a hill, but not the same hill we were on.

We had to hike around a mountain edge that connected the opposing hills over some very steep terrain and in some cases very close to a cliff. If you knew me you would also know that I do not like heights.

When we were coming into position, some farm workers came looking for cattle and the kudus disappeared into those hills. By now, I was quite ready for some "No-Bwana" game.

In the afternoon, we got to a new place hunting for blesbok and impala and happened to come across impala first.

Again, if the impala were not on a hill, we were, and this time, we had to climb down for the stalk on a bachelor's herd. During the more or less two hour stalk, we watched some of the rams fighting, probably for the (male only) herd domain. It was amazing how the impala sounded like enraged hogs during their dispute.

We (or I) ended the chase with a single shot on the shoulder/neck area at 170 meters but I am not sure how happy Frans and Munguezi were since they had to carry that impala ram out for quite some distance until they reached a point the truck could reach.

Day 3 31 May 2005 (Great View)

Back on the same spot as yesterday for kudu. This time, we had a soft hike only, no real climbing, but again, no kudu. Since it was Mongezi's call to come back, here this occasion is now known as "Mongezi's Kudu."

Back to the lodge, brunch and we go out for blesbok around the same place we got the impala yesterday. Very soon, we spot blesbok, many blesbok, and the stalk starts.

I must say that I became very intimate with my PH Frans today. We crawled for almost three hours (it was an over five hour stalk) on our hands and knees, and the most prevalent view I had during this time was Frans' ass.

After spotting a very large ram, we lost him just before we could get into shooting position. Then we were spotted by a mountain reedbuck doe that would not let us go (or continue our hunt). By the end of the day we were surrounded by almost 40 female blesboks and not a single ram to bag. Life!

Coming back to the truck, we saw a nice kudu bull that just disappeared in the dusk.

Day 4 01 June 2005 (New Acquaintances)

New PH (Stuart) and additional tracker (Lucas) and mixed feelings. We started early for kudu in the main lodge property. Early on our stalk, we are spotted by a small herd of red hartebeest and they, in turn, spook the kudu.

We continue to stalk (or climb) for kudu and when we come to a place just over a hill where kudu are barking all around I slip on the trail, fall down, and put a nice scratch on my rifle scope.

Suddenly, all the kudu in the world are on my sights but I never had a shot at a mature bull. Immature bulls, horns that did not complete two full curls, cows, yearlings, you figure it. Once we had a nice bull broadside at around 400 meters, but he was completely surrounded by cows and that was too far out anyways.

Back to lodge, brunch and common or cape springbok in the afternoon.

And we had all the animal species in the concession surrounding us, except the one we were after, springbok. Finally, a chance, a dominant male is broadside at 250 meters. I shoot over it. I should mention that this was the only shot that I heard the noise and felt the recoil during the entire hunt and therefore, I believe I anticipated the shot and flinched.

Late afternoon we go out for more kudu. Downhill, uphill. The sun goes down. No kudu. Deception.

Day 5 02 June 2005 (Battery Charge)

Today is my wife's birthday and I must have good news by the time I call her.

We started early for gemsbok or oryx and cape springbok in another concession—Malanskraal—and spotted a gemsbok herd from the truck where the bush meets the grass.

We had a good hour crawling on our hands and knees to come to a good shooting position, leaning against a tree some 170 meters from the undisturbed herd. Stalking a herd like this is a good exercise on learning how predators like lions approach a herd. We move against the wind and only when the wind is blowing so the prey cannot scent us or detect strange movements on the grass.

Stuart points out an old male and when I take the shot he drops down in his tracks, spined. We come in close and put a finishing shot at about 10 paces, the only one needed so far. The old Gemsbok had almost no teeth left and in a very short time, he would start to have problems eating, become weak and face the slow death of herbivores in a world without large predators.

As we drive back to have the gemsbok skinned, we spot several small herds of cape springbok, both common and white (a melanistic variation like the Black Springbok) on the flat grasslands and they are wild and smart enough to keep at least 500 meters between then and us. We learned later that this place is often hunted by meat or "biltong" hunters, and that they do the shooting from vehicles. This non-sportive and unethical behavior should also be illegal.

Although killing is an important part of hunting, it must not be a synonym to hunt. Ethical behavior and fair chase are key factors that differentiate hunters from killers and Theodore Roosevelt said "the finding and killing of the game is after all but a part of the whole."

When we dropped the gemsbok off, we found some more unpleasant leftovers from the so-called "biltong hunters", several heads of immature kudu bulls, animals that never had a chance to become an unforgettable trophy, their image forever etched on the hunter's memory.

After a snack, we continue the chase for springbok and had a relatively easy hands and knees stalk (I am becoming an expert by now) over open land. We must take advantage of every patch of grass, gentle slopes and any foot-high anthills.

A very fine ram falls down to a should-neck shot at 220 meters.

More pictures, as usual, and we drive back to the lodge for brunch and kudu in the afternoon.

A common theme in Africa is that, generally, we see all the animals we are not looking for but not the particular one we desire; in my case, a mature Kudu bull with well-developed horns. This afternoon, we saw blue wildebeest, impala, red hartebeest, springbok and more.

As we were seating under the shade of an acacia thorn bush, two kudu cows come less than 10 meters from us. They flick their ears, bark and as we don't move, leave quietly, returning to spy on us again after several minutes. Then we move up another hill and continue our stalk.

Several kudu cows and a very large bull are at shooting distance but, as fate follows me, the bull has a single if very long horn.

More fruitless stalking and when it is too dark for anything else, we start going down and my left knee gives up so I must use the shooting sticks to help me climb down.

Day 6 03 June 2005 (Two bad legs)

My left knee is still hurting but we go up another mountain for kudu. The morning is too warm and they are already way up the opposing hills. We then decide to go over our hill to spot the other side.

No kudu but some black wildebeest, one standing apart from the others, an old bull with a broken leg, probably the result of a fight over breeding rights. The stuff life is made of.

Another hill to climb down and my knee gets worse. I trade my rifle for the shooting sticks again. Midway down, I break one of the shooting stick legs. Now I have a walking stick and it is surprising how much it helps.

We stalk the bull to 80 meters but he does not give us a shot and suddenly runs away. We decided to continue to chase him and that means another hill to climb and hard use for my new walking stick.

From the flat top of the next hill, we see the bull at about 200 meters almost staring at us. I ease my rifle against a broken tree branch and wait. Patience is not one of my few virtues and 10 minutes may sometimes look like 10 days. Finally, the bull turns broadside and I shoot a little bit too far back but still hit both lungs.

Pugh, Stuart's short-legged Jack Russell Terrier, goes strong in the blood spoor but there is enough blood on the ground for almost anyone to track it. She also does a great job in helping preparing the trophies for the photo sessions by leaking the blood from the shot wounds and nostrils. It looks like the PHs are very fond of this small dogs for tracking wounded animals.

We found the wildebeest less than 100 meters from where he was shot, broken leg and all.

I could never have a black wildebeest shoulder mounted. That face, the hair coming straight above the nostrils, would cause nightmares to my family and my son would visit our bed quite more often than he currently does.

The bull dropped very close to a road and I told our trackers that I planned the lung shot so it would be easier to get the wildebeest on the truck.

I also kept my rifle very close at hand. Since we shot that particular bull due to his bad leg, I did not want anyone to do me any favors.

As for the rest of the day, there was more climbing, more stalking, zebra, giraffes, impala, warthog, but no kudu.

Tonight we went out for dinner at, what I believe is, the only restaurant in Adelaide (there is also only one gas station). I had T-bone steak.

Day 7 04 June 2005 (The way hunting should be)

This may be a little too early to write about this day but I must do it now. As I write, I am seated by a fireplace enjoying the "*dolce fa niente*" of a Sunday morning on safari.

When we first got to camp and started to discuss over dinner what we expected and what to expect of safari, Frans mentioned that Kudu was always the most elusive and difficult animal to hunt, taking his clients an average of seven days.

After hunting intensively for kudu many hours a day, mornings and afternoons, for six days and having all kinds of feelings about Hemingway and Ruark's exasperations over kudu, or the grey ghost, especially after Randy came back to camp with a nice bull on the second day (seven days average...bah!) and not having a shot opportunity at any trophy animal, I was starting to consider writing and drinking, in any particular order, as the best cure for kudu anguish as my aforementioned heroes did.

By the way, Frans was quick to point out that the main problem that both Mr. Hemingway and Mr. Ruark had with kudu hunting was that both gentlemen dedicated more time and attention to the gin bottle than to kudu. Or so is said in Africa.

But let's get back to the hunt. As usual, we got up early, around 5:00 AM, did the normal things that are expected to be done on every safari like having a very light breakfast of very hot tea and toasts or rusks, the hard South African bread with sugar and raisins that may break your teeth if you don't dip it in your tea or coffee, grabbed our gear, got on the 4X4 and drove to Oliphant Bosch (Elephant Forest), the last place elephants roamed free around the Eastern Cape region before they were shot out in the 1850-1860s.

We are after bushbuck, the green-eyed devil (since the first one I shot had only one horn, Frans told me that I could take a second bushbuck) and just to keep up with tradition, we start our hunt by climbing a hill. As it was the case in the last couple days, I carry my now inseparable walking stick. My knees need help.

This was a cold morning with frost on the ground and bushbucks were expected to come out and warm up at first light. After glassing the opposing hills, Stuart and the trackers, Lucas and Andelay, decide that we must move elsewhere to get better advantage of the coming sun.

We do so and, after a while, spot several young bushbucks and then see a nice mature male. I put my scope cross-hairs on the animal and then wait about a half hour (an eternity) until he comes out of the bushes and into a clearing. He goes down immediately from a shoulder-spine-lungs shot at about 200 meters.

Following the usual photo session and field dressing, we drive up the mountain range searching for blesbok on the grasslands on top of the plateaus where we could again see the Winterberg on the horizon.

As we were coming to the top, the trackers spotted a sizeable herd. We leave the truck and start stalking. We walk for a short distance, go down to our hands and knees and finally proceed belly crawling as there are no trees up the plateau and only the short grass hides us.

Stuart singles out a nice ram and points him out to me. I bring him in my sights and as the blesbok looks backwards, Stuart asks me to shoot where his nose touches his body. At 250 meters, my shot hits that precise spot and the ram never moves anywhere but down.

The warm sun and the cold mountain air are so inviting that I just sit and write some of this journal for over an hour on the grassy slope.

We drive to Frans' farm and spend a couple hours skinning and capping the bushbuck and the blesbok and then drive off again to another range where Stuart prepared a gorgeous meal while I had a good hour sleep under the African sun. Blesbok liver wrapped in bacon, sausages, eggs, baked beans, cheese and fresh mushrooms with some honey mustard. A banquet.

At about 3:30 PM, we start after kudu again. The difference this time is that we start by climbing downhill which seems to be worse on my knees. We come to a ridge and start glassing, or more accurately, they start glassing and I try to hold my hat against the strong wind.

Stuart spots a couple nice kudu bulls about one kilometer away (don't ask me how, training I would guess) and we take on the chase. As we move closer, we must worry not only about the kudu but about other animals as well. Suddenly, a warthog dashes away with his tail held high like an antenna and not long after that a duiker jumps out just to disappear in seconds in the next thick bush.

Now we are going uphill and as we close on the kudus (two bulls, one young male, two or three cows) the adrenalin rushes in and I completely forget the pain on my knees.

Stuart stops, sets the shooting sticks, I point my rifle and can't see anything but bushes. Then, as if in a dream, the grey ghost materializes, apart from the cows and the young male, inside a thick bush I see the ivory tips of my kudu's horns, then the white chevron on his nose, the ears, and the mane under his neck.

By this time, probably disturbed by the noise my heart is making, he moves out from his hiding place. I pin the cross hairs to his left shoulder and at 280 meters squeeze the trigger.

The shot hits a little low and he walks away to my despair but soon falls down. We move closer and I put a final heart shot at 150 meters while he is lying down, clearly sick, with blood dropping from his nostrils.

I cannot describe all the feelings that invaded me when I first approached and then touched and hugged that magnificent animal. Exhilaration.

As dusk approaches, we rush the photo session and finish capping my kudu under torch lights and then I am submitted to my first kudu ritual (also known as the "Dumb Bwana Ritual"). My face is smeared with my kudu's blood and I must eat a piece of its liver. Andile looks even more cheerful than his usual friendly state.

Why not? A safari is the realization of personal fantasies and dreams and it must be as enjoyable and memorable as one makes it. *Carpe diem.*

Day 8 05 June 2005 (Resting)

I decided not to hunt this morning and write about yesterday. Kudu is such a symbolic animal and an achievement that I need time to absorb him, to savor him, to digest him, but by midday, temptation overcomes me and I wander around the lodge with a shotgun. I shoot one turtle neck dove in a most nice shot, even if I do say so.

After brunch, I spent most of the afternoon in bed, most likely rejoicing about my kudu, the most beautiful animal I ever touched. Late in the afternoon, we go out looking for buffalo and locate them just before dusk.

Initially, we hear the buffalo trumping the vegetation in the bottom of a ravine, the only animal so far that did not care about the noise it makes, then the sounds die, and suddenly, not 20 meters away, appears the herd dominant bull, sniffing the air, looking for us.

I had never been stalked by an animal before and the fact that we were up the ravine, close to the 4x4, and that I had my 30-06 rifle with me did not made me that much more comfortable. Those impressive black horns, extended nostrils, mud covered back that gives the pitch black bull a false silver color, transmit an image of such primitive brutality and danger that it brought to my mind the thought of how fragile a man can be.

The 30-06 that had put to ground nine animals in the first shot was now as underpowered as an air gun. I decided, and this time I am certain that my wife will agree with me, that I must buy a .458 Winchester Magnum or bigger rifle just in case buffalo come to visit us one day.

Day 9 06 June 2005 (Being Lazy)

We go out hunting pro-forma only. If an exceptional animal shows up I will consider taking it, otherwise just an easy walk in the morning not to abuse my knee. We stalk some fallow deer but because the buck is nothing more than average, we let him go.

I am still enjoying a sensation of accomplishment and don't really want to kill anything today.

On the way back to the lodge, I buy a knife for my collection and chat with the gun store owner. He tells me that in over 18 months, he has not sold a single firearm due to the new regulations being put in place in the Republic of South Africa. This brings my thoughts back home to Brazil and to how people can make stupid decisions based on apparently good intentions.

I sleep and read in the afternoon and then we go see the giraffes before sunset.

Day 10 07 June 2005 (Saying Good-Bye)

In the morning, we visited the Mpolo Game Reserve, about an hour away from our lodge, but still we could see the Winterberg's flat top and scarps.

The most amazing sight was the white rhino. First, an absolutely large male with great horns and then a group of females and young males that, after seeing us, took to an impressive defensive formation. All tails together and the horns out in a perfect five pointed star.

We had lunch at the Adelaide hotel. Frans, Stuart, Randy and I then went back to the lodge and this journal.

The wind picks up and a storm appears to be forming and I wonder if this wind also didn't happen just before Adam was expelled from the Garden of Eden or Hemingway from the Green Hills of Africa!

We leave Africa tomorrow and will fly west with the night.

Chasing Cougar Over 30 Years

Imagine a child that wants to take possession of a treasure, and as simple as a child's treasure can be, they can be unachievable, owned by giants, guarded by tradition.

Imagine now that same child, having crossed oceans, explored continents, still loving the same giants, and unsuspecting of the passing of time, suddenly coming across the once much-desired treasure.

I already told you about the farm house I grew up in and about the 1960s vintage cabinet that was in the front guest room and some of the treasures that it contained. One of them was a paper box that once encased a hunting knife.

Ivete was a close friend to my mother that sometimes would visit us at the farm. She worked at the "Casa Bardaro" in Ribeirão Preto, a very traditional hardware and home appliances store that did not survive the turbulent evolution of the Brazilian economy during the 1980s.

On one of her visits in the early 1970s, Ivete presented my father, who at the time was a dedicated outdoorsman, with a hunting knife. This knife was made by Mundial, a large Brazilian cutlery that, unfortunately, no longer makes sport knives, and had a design inspired on some Puma skinners and was aptly named Cougar.

Although a cougar is a puma by any other name and vice-versa, this Cougar knife had a distinct personality. The blade is forged from high-carbon steel and then hard chromed, the handles or scales are some kind of Brazilian hardwood and a long leather tong passed through an eye on the tang. A leather sheath accompanied the knife. I remember an occasion when my father took this knife on a duck hunt and lost it on his way back to the truck and then backtracked through the swamp until he found it.

If the Cougar knife was attractive, its paper case was fascinating. On the cover, there was a picture of a high-power, bolt-action, scoped rifle with set triggers and some bottlenecked cartridges on top of a jaguar or leopard pelt.

All these things were rare and exotic for a child in my situation. Brazilian gun laws being restrictive as they have always been and American or African big-spotted cats also not being available around the corner (not that there were many street corners on the farm) made my imagination take off. Compound that with a healthy dose of Tarzan comic books, movies and stories generously supplied by my grandfather and you may see me flying from our farm to the jungles of Mato Grosso and from there to the savannahs of Africa.

But children are careless with their treasures and one day that box disappeared and the knife submerged in some obscure kitchen duty as the years went by.

Just before Christmas of 1999, we visited our family farm in Goiás state, central Brazil, just weeks before I relocated to the Netherlands with my wife and children and as I snooped around drawers and cabinets, I found that Cougar knife, rusted, broken tip, but never forgotten. I took it to the tool shop, cleaned all the rust, reshaped the blade and sharpened it until it could cut as well as a cougar can bite and let my father know I had taken possession of a treasure.

During the short three years that we lived in the Netherlands, I used the Cougar intensively, special on barbecues and when we again relocated to the United States, it came along with us.

But since the world is full of surprises, this story is not over yet.

One Saturday on the summer of 2004, I was looking around at things at a gun show in Kalamazoo, Michigan, when coming on to a table, I saw a card box with the picture of a high-power, scoped rifle and some bottlenecked cartridges on top of a jaguar or leopard pelt and inside it, a brand new Cougar knife.

After asking for the price of the knife, I paid the amount so fast I must have frightened the seller. I had to be quick or the Cougar could get away.

Clearly, that gentleman did not know that he had a treasure on his hands. A treasure that, after 30 years, is finally mine.

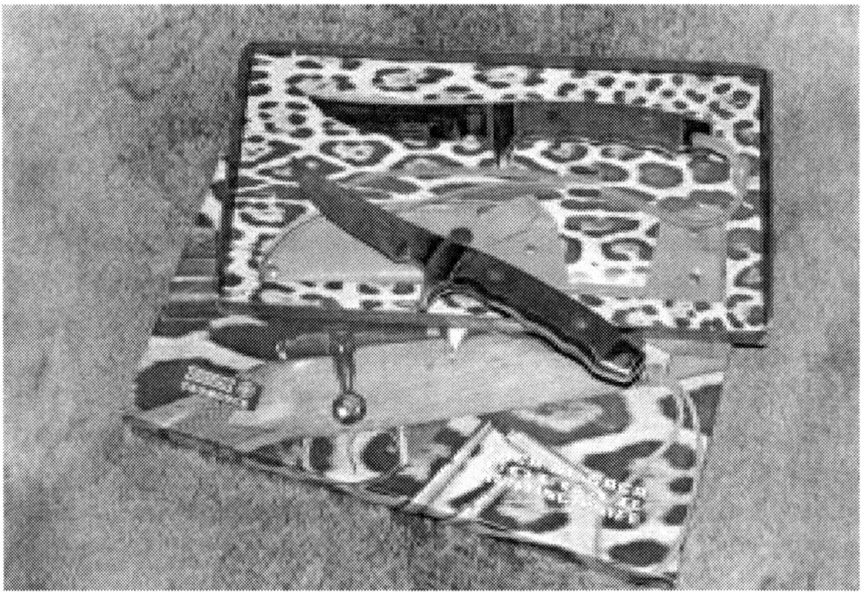

The Roads of Politics or the Politics of Roads

My great grandfather, Magino Diniz Junqueira, did not get along with his brother Orlando, to put it in mild terms.

It was never clear to me why they had a problem and the matter was never really discussed in the family but it had something to do with politics and we knew that death threats had taken place and that there was a certain .44 caliber Winchester rifle kept loaded on top of my great grandfather's wardrobe.

Now it is important to take things in perspective; rural Brazil before WWII, even in the more developed São Paulo state with its endless coffee plantations, was a completely different universe than what we are used to today. The big coffee farmers, coffee barons, had a lot of influence and "political responsibilities" and a word spoken was a life commitment and when a relationship turned sour, even between brothers, there were no comebacks.

Great Grandpa Magino, using his own resources, built two roads in our region, from Morro Agudo to São Joaquim da Barra and from Orlândia to Guaíra, both nowadays paved and important for the region's economy. It is said that his brother, Orlando, sent some of his employees to change some part of the road design, a certain underground cattle passage, just by my grandfather's pharmacy in the Peroba farm and that Magino, on horseback and in arms, ran them away, unharmed, but scared with some unkind message to his brother.

Such incidents did not to improve the family relations or the local politics.

In that time, and up to my childhood, the farms had large colonies where the workers and their families lived, and at the Fazenda Peroba, my great grandfather's over-a-million-coffee-tree-plantation, the colony population was at something over two thousand people, including families and single employees.

Tropical diseases, especially malaria and yellow fever, were then extremely common and great grandmother, D. Maria de Paula, kept an infirmary in her house basement to treat employees and one of the sickbeds was almost directly underneath the master bedroom's wardrobe.

Now, we all know how curious children are, and Gabriel Euclides, the youngest brother of my grandmother and better known to us as Tio Bié, a certain day wanted to see his father gun, the Winchester rifle. A young child at the time, he climbed the wardrobe and as he tried to bring the gun down he dropped it barrel first on the wooden floor, and to general surprise as the barrel hit the ground a shot came out of it, going through the floor as well as the sickbed in the basement.

The sick employee on that bed was saved because at the moment of the shot he was having a bowl of soup, sitting on the bed instead of laying on it.

Needless to say, that young Bié went through quite a spanking, the standard pedagogic treatment of the time and no one else was worse for the experience.

By the way, the political misunderstanding was never solved between the brothers. When his brother Orlando passed away, my great grandfather ordered his hounds released, grabbed his hat and went out hunting.

And two or three generations later we would still not discuss politics among the family branches, even when one of the roads Great Grandpa Magino built was named after his brother, Orlando.

Alligators in the Sky

Besides being very tasty, alligators (and for the matter, crocodiles) are fascinating animals. They are successful predators, extremely adaptable, can survive for months without food, but can feed on almost any form of animal protein or tissue, and have an envious characteristic: the older the males get, the more fertile and sexually active they are.

All my alligator experiences run around one or another of the smaller species of the Brazilian *jacaré* or Cayman as it is known elsewhere. The largest Brazilian alligator, the *jacaré-açu* (the Tupi Indian name means "big lizard"), is only found in the Amazon River system, and can reach up to six meters (around 18 feet) in length, comparable to the Nile and salt-water crocodiles.

I remember when I was around five years old and an alligator was caught on a "wait-hook" on a lake in our farm. A "wait-hook" is a sort of a trap, quite illegal nowadays (at least in Brazil), made of a large hook or spoon cast to a good two feet steel leader, a swivel, and then a length of strong line tied to a flexible tree limb or branch. The flexible branch is a necessary measure to avoid snapping the line. "Wait-hooks" are generally used for large nocturnal fish but the odd alligator may eventually find them.

I must tell you that I only saw that alligator by midmorning, after it had been gutted and the excellent tail meat taken away, but the large open mouth and the fresh-in-my-mind Tarzan comic books were enough to inspire a great degree of respect for the animal.

Mr. Candinho, the same gentleman that several years later would shoot a rather large anaconda that had my father by his hand, wanted to show us the alligator teeth or perhaps he just wanted to retrieve the spoon still hooked to the powerful jaw. As he fingered around the large head the alligator, as if alive, snapped its jaws shut and took a bite out of one of Mr. Candinho's fingers. It may not have been as traumatic a loss as Captain Hook's but, pardon the pun, a hook cost a portion of his finger.

That experience was enough to make me understand that alligators may be easy to kill but are quite hard to die.

Several years later, along with my cousin Marco Aurélio, I went on my first alligator hunt, in the swamps of my family farm—Fazenda Taboa— and as we did not have a boat, we had to improvise. We got a tractor wheel inner tube, filled it with air and put a wooden plank over it for a seat, and used a long pole for propulsion and steering along with our feet.

Unhappily or not, except for an unsuccessful shot at a passing duck, we never had the opportunity to fight and defeat any monstrous lizard. The two mighty hunters probably scared them away or most likely, the alligators were too busy laughing at the two quixotes.

In a certain June, after I returned from six months in the United States as an exchange student I went on a two week fishing trip to Mato Grosso, in the fringes of the Brazilian Legal Amazon. We stayed at the São Jorge Preto farm that belonged to my uncles Amaury and Marcelinho. We drove in two Chevrolet pick-ups, my father, my brother Rodolfo, Mr. Jaime Faváro in one and Uncle Amaury, José Aleixo, better known as "Zé da Brucelose" and me on the other. From our home town we drove to Barra do Garça, on the banks of the Araguaia River, and from there to the farm, in the São José do Xingu municipality, better known as "Bang" or "São José do Bang Bang". You can figure why.

The trip itself took around 34 hours driving, the last 400 kilometers (250 miles) accounting for over ten hours, and to get to the farm we totaled five burst tires between the two trucks.

North Mato Gross is frontier country as wild as or even more wild than remote parts of Alaska, Canada or Africa. During summer or the rain season, from October to March, the roads are impassable and even the bush planes may face problem as the dirt runways start to soften. During winter, or the dry season, roads are drivable but an unpredictable dry fog may ground anything that does not have a GPS, satellite navigation or common sense.

When you go there, prepare yourself, for the closest gas stations may be anything from a three hours drive to a day or so. Of course, you could call a plane as long as your radio worked, you could afford it and the plane could find where you are.

This trip was a totally new experience for me, demanding sometimes (having to manage my father away from mother), but mostly exciting.

We fished the Comandante Fontoura, a slow-flowing, dark water river, with the luxuriant tropical jungle suffocating its margins. As it was too hot during the day, we generally started fishing around 4PM and kept going to midnight or later. Those nights floating on this river provided some of the most fascinating moments I had in the outdoors.

The tropical sky is incomparable in the amount of stars and the clear and cool winter nights, so far away from any city or pollution let those stars shine with such power against the dark night that they looked like diamonds under a powerful spotlight. The Milky Way or Via Láctea, as we say in Brazil, floated in the night sky just like the river we floated in cut the heartlands of Brazil and several times, I wondered where we were floating, on the river or on the sky.

But suddenly, I would be brought back to the earth, or better yet, to the river, as the long shadows of the alligators would silently swim among the stars under our boat with slow strokes from their powerful tails.

Only in Africa on safari did I see a sky that could perhaps compare to Brazil; deep darkness and brilliant stars with the Southern Cross to guide me around.

I shot one alligator during that trip and my father cooked it while we were still there. I absolutely love the taste and consistency of alligator meat, it reminds me of lobster.

Also, during that trip I had one of the biggest scares of my life. One day my father decided to go out only with my brother and me. We packed the bare essentials and would have lunch on whatever we fished. That was a very poor day and the only fish we caught was a rather large black piranha. We made a fire on a clearing and cooked it the Indian way, on a grill made of green branches above hot coals. We were either very hungry or the piranha was delicious, probably both, but my father didn't eat even a small piece.

After the meal, we continued fishing and were as unlucky as before and finally, late at night, we, actually my father, decided it was time to go back to camp, and as he pulled the starting cord on the outboard motor, he did not notice that it was in gear. When the engine started it sent the boat swirling around and my father lost his balance, and went overboard, hitting his kidney on the board on his way to the water.

I am still not sure how my, at the time, little and skinny brother and I hauled our father back into the boat but all the jungle creatures, alligators, anacondas, piranhas, mermaids, were very polite and did not disturb us in the process.

The following year, I went to college and many years would go by before I could play with alligators again. But as it happened, that was, so far, the last time I was in the outdoors with my father and brothers.

We went to fish the Crixá-Mirim River in northern Goiás state and stayed at the Fazenda Ronda that belongs to Uncle Maninho, my brother Rogério's godfather, and due to work, I was there only for the weekend but wanted to have at least one alligator (many times my stomach rules me).

On the first night in camp, we went out for alligator, three in a six meter (18 feet) aluminum boat, waiting for the search light to reflect on their eyes just above water. Jesus, our farm manager, got excited and took a shot at the first gator he saw, which swam away. He probably missed completely as 12 gauge buckshot is more than enough gun for even quite large lizards but as I could not be sure about it, we followed the alligator and I killed the only three foot long animal with a head shot from my .38 revolver.

As that alligator was too small to feed all the eight or ten people in camp, we went after another one and I was to shoot first this time.

The .38 Special, hard-cast, wad-cutter bullet is the most efficient alligator medicine I ever used. When the flat point hits the animal's skull, it shatters the bone plates to pieces and the shock kills the animal immediately. I never saw an alligator move after being hit by it in the head, except for starting to think slowly.

Now, you must remember that it is not because you killed an alligator that it is dead. Even with the brains blown out, you must be careful in handling the animal and danger can come from either end, mouth or tail.

I have never been comfortable with a loaded long gun, be it a shotgun or rifle, on a small boat. There are no racks or any place to hold it properly and its always banging around, getting wet and its muzzle pointing at something, or worse, someone. The nice thing about a pistol is that I can keep it holstered and safe until the boat gets within a few feet of the alligator and I always know exactly where the muzzle is pointing when I am handling it.

Shortly after, we found a larger alligator and it was almost too easy. I steered the boat towards it, cut the engine, and shot at its head no more that a couple yards away. The dinner-to-be never moved a scale, and I hooked it as it started to sink.

I had several more encounters with alligators, most quite uneventful to tell you about; a boat in the night, two or three people in it, one shot, one alligator. But the closest I ever came to any harm was with 12 inch long alligator. That was one of three baby alligators that someone captured and left for some days in a tank in our farm to show to children.

When I brought my children to visit the small animals, they were quite shy and tried to hide under some vegetation in the tank. As I did not want my children to be disappointed I grabbed one of the little alligators and he slipped through my grip and bit my opposite hand. My pride was hurt more than my hand but I carried the elongated semicircular marks in the skin for a couple weeks.

Blue Collar Pigeons

In one of the very first articles I wrote, I tried to present the notion of game and vermin (or varmint) and some of the reason to hunt animals from both groups, and mentioned that certain animals could be classified as either game or vermin depending on their scarcity and their impact on human activity (a polite way to say how much annoyance any given animal causes to us).

As time passes and my comprehension of the human mind diminishes, I see that we tend to classify as vermin some animals that share a very human characteristic: adaptability (Man is the most adaptable living being on Earth and the only creature that inhabits all continents and latitudes). Some animals that are classified as vermin today have a very long relationship to man, and followed us in our migrations around the world (or more specifically from Europe to the rest of the world): rats, pigs, sparrows and the literal target of this story, the domestic pigeon (*Columba livia*).

Another concept that we must introduce before getting into this story is that of a feral animal or an animal that is wild but originated from domestic stock. In all cases that I am aware of, feral animal are alien species introduced by man into a new habitat and that started to interact to this new habitat beyond human control. Classic examples happened with mammals in Australia (rabbits, goats, pigs, water buffalo, camels, you name it), pigs (or boars) in the United Stated and Brazil, raccoons in Germany, nutrias in France and the Netherlands, and almost everywhere, the domestic pigeon.

The poor domestic pigeon is called, by most people that don't feed them, a rat with wings, a nuisance that stain public monuments, spreads diseases and damages property with their droppings and nests, a vermin by any classification. But, one must at least recognize that the domestic pigeon can be a very beautiful bird and quite a strong flier, two qualities that appeal to the hunter.

In the beginning of my professional career, I worked for around two years at a fertilizer plant in the outskirts of Campinas, a large city about 100 kilometers due north of São Paulo, Brazil. As fertilizers are very corrosive all the roofing on the buildings was made of wood structure. The free space between the roof frame and the singles made for perfect nesting spots and the pigeons put it to good use.

The pigeon population was so high that they became a good reason to request everyone, including visitors, to wear hard hats, as we never knew when or where their droppings would hit someone.

Sometime after I left that company, I got a call from a friend, Mr. Moisés, telling me that the plant foreman was really unhappy about the pigeons and asking whether I would like to help them to manage the problem and if I could provide the tools. I agreed to help and we scheduled action for the next Sunday in order to have a quiet time.

Early in the afternoon of a gorgeous winter day, blue spotless sky, warm sun and cool shades, I met Mr. Moisés and we drove to the plant main building, selected our tools and got ready to start our cleaning operation.

I used a Feinwerkbau Model 65 recoilless spring-piston air pistol with custom target grips that was used to set a South American 10 meter air pistol record that stood up for almost 20 years. This gun is a precision tool that out-shoots me everyday of the week and twice on Sunday and is designed to put 10 shots through a single hole at the 10 meters regulation distance. It has precise adjustable sights, crispy trigger that broke at well under a pound, and a barrel-slide assembly that would travel freely on the frame to neutralize any recoil you could have when the lead pellet went out of the barrel at a constant 535 feet per second. I measured that pistol muzzle velocity on different occasions and it never changed.

Mr. Moisés used a Brazilian-made spring-piston break barrel air rifle by CBC (Companhia Brasileira de Cartuchos), the parent company of Magtech. Although not as sophisticated as the Feinwerkbau, the little rifle served its purpose well.

It took us some minutes to get used to the very steep angles we had to shoot in order to hit the pigeons without endangering people or equipment. As we were inside a building, we took no shots at less than a 45 degree angle and we took many shots straight up (90 degrees). Now, you must remember that we were using low-power air guns shooting soft, pure lead pellets. Even at low speeds these pellets will smash against any hard surface and will never ricochet. The point here is hard surfaces, concrete, brick and mortar or hard wood. Don't try shooting air guns (or any firearm) unless you have a proper backstop.

The best kill shots were straight up. We would locate a nest and stand below it and the roosting birds were just too curious. As they would stretch their necks to look at us we would pick their heads on our sights and press the trigger. In most cases they balanced forward and gravity would bring them down.

There were so many birds and we got such a cadence that I believe that I averaged about a bird a minute and Mr. Moisés was not far behind that, and at the end of an hour or so, we had a wheel-barrel full of multicolored pigeons.

As the main culling was successful, we decided to concentrate only on the more challenging shots and enjoy the hunt. By the next hour, each of us had shot more than twenty or thirty birds and some shots were well beyond 40 yards. Most of them were clean, one-shot kills.

Some birds were claimed by the resident cats and we shared others with employees on duty. The lion's share we took to Mr. Moisés' home where we shared the best part of the harvest with his neighbors and plugged and drawn our share while sipping cold beer and remembering the best moments of the day.

As you can imagine, by sunset, shots were longer and the pigeons prettier and bigger, probably looking like pheasants.

Although some people may criticize the number of birds we bagged on a single afternoon it is important to point out that no bird went to waste and that our shooting was much cleaner than some of the nuisance animal management alternatives, such as poison, besides being extremely cost effective for both hunters and landlords. We didn't pay or charge anything and still had a wonderful time almost outdoors.

Shotguning My Way

A shotgun is the most versatile firearm a person can own and use and I believe that any person with any involvement with the outdoors should have at least one. By the very nature of being able to shoot from the smallest shot to a single heavy slug a shotgun can theoretically be used to hunt anything from a sparrow to an elephant (although I would not recommend that you try the latter), and be used for sport, police and military duties, survival and self-defense.

My first gun was an 8 mm (.310") rim fire single shot break open shotgun made by CBC (Companhia Brasileira de Cartuchos) and it was responsible to start a love affair or at least an infatuation with shotguns that spans for over 30 years, at least a dozen smoothbore firearms, and the opportunity to use them in four very different countries: Brazil, the Netherlands, the United States and South Africa.

But my memory brings me back to long before I had my first gun. I was quite young, three, maybe four years old, when I followed my father and his English pointer, Diana, while they hunted "codorna" (*Notura maculosa*), a local, tailless partridge that offers both superior sport and table fare. My father always used a side-by-side 28 gauge shotgun and

I would aim to gather one or more of the spent green shells.

There is no better smell in the world than the inebriant essence of a fired shotgun shell, especially if it is one of the old waxed paper hulls. Just the other day after coming back from a short hunt with my Black Lab, Tupã, I found some fired shells in my pocket while talking to my wife and my sister-in-law. As I smelled the delicate fragrance, I traveled in time and space to the vanished meadows and picked corn fields of my childhood, walking after my father.

We lived on a farm, and money was a very rare commodity. Factory ammo was expensive and difficult to come by; therefore, reloading was not only an option, but almost a necessity. My father would gather some of our decades-long farm employees and his trusted hunt companions and reload several boxes of 28 gauge shells. The process was quite labor intensive, as was much of the farming activities in Brazil at the time. The first step was to use a punch and a hammer and cut felt and cardboard wads. Each shell required one felt and three cardboard wads, and each wad required at least one hammer blow, so there was probably as much noise in making a shell as in discharging it.

The next step was to de-prime and then re-prime the shells, and that also took some hammering, at least to remove the old primer. Then gun powder was poured in the hull. I remember clearly that we used "Pólvora Química Tupã" (Tupã Chemical Powder) and you may guess any connection or coincidence between that powder and my dog's name. Tupã is the god of thunder for one of the major Brazilian Indian nation and is a very appropriate name for gun powder. Tupã powder came in a small, light blue, plastic bottle (100 grams or 3.5 ounces per bottle) with white lettering and the caricature of a hunter stepping over a knocked out jaguar while holding its tail in one hand and having a large bowie knife in his belt.

And finally came the shot, an overshot wad and the hull received a roll crimp in a small hand-powered tool.

When I was finally allowed to hunt by myself, I used the small 310 to hunt doves, pigeons, and tinamous or using their proper names Juriti (*Leptotila varreaux*), Azulega (*Columba cayennensis*) and Inhanbú-chitã (*Cryptellus parvirostris*). I must confess that I was never an accomplished wing shooter during my early years and that I would stalk those birds just as I stalked big game in Africa many decades later. Locate the prey by sight or sound and sneak close enough for the diminutive load of number 11 shot to be effective. The 310 shell is about the same size as a .32 S&W Long revolver cartridge so there is not much payload there to play with.

While the seed of the blood sport was present in my hunt, so was the basic instinct of the predator, and not one of those birds were ever spoiled, unless you consider bad cooking as spoiling good game birds.

I also used that 310 as an effective replacement for a fishing rod, and I didn't even need line and hook. As you may have guessed by now, I deeply enjoy hunting, the chase and the outsmarting of the prey, but I am still working on refining my taste for fishing. The *Rosário* creek that cuts the farm I was raised in, at one point makes a pronounced S-shaped curve where, at an outer part of the curve, the slow waters form a shallow beach. Touching the shallow waters there was a pig sty and the bagres (*Bagre spp.*), a kind of Brazilian catfish, would come to feed on pig manure. I would stay out of sight under some shade tree with other kids, and when the foot-long fish would come in the shallows waters I just had to shoot at it and one of us would wade in to retrieve our prize.

By late afternoon, we would gather our daily bag of fish and fowl, find some discarded kitchen oil can, there were some rectangular peanut oil cans that made wonderful fry pans when opened properly, and hide among the banana trees where we would make a small fire from the huge dry leaves. Then we would cook and consume our wonderful harvest without having to share it with grown-ups.

Big game hunting is challenging and rewarding and I am blessed to have the opportunity to do it, but I can get no better enjoyment than scouting the woods and meadows for small game with a small gauge shotgun, be it for tinamou in Brazil or cottontail rabbit in Michigan.

And speaking of small gauge shotguns, as I grew up and wanted to hunt larger animals, I graduated from the 310 to an old Rossi 28 gauge side-by-side shotgun with external hammers. Although, technically a small gauge shotgun, when I first started using the 28 I felt like I was

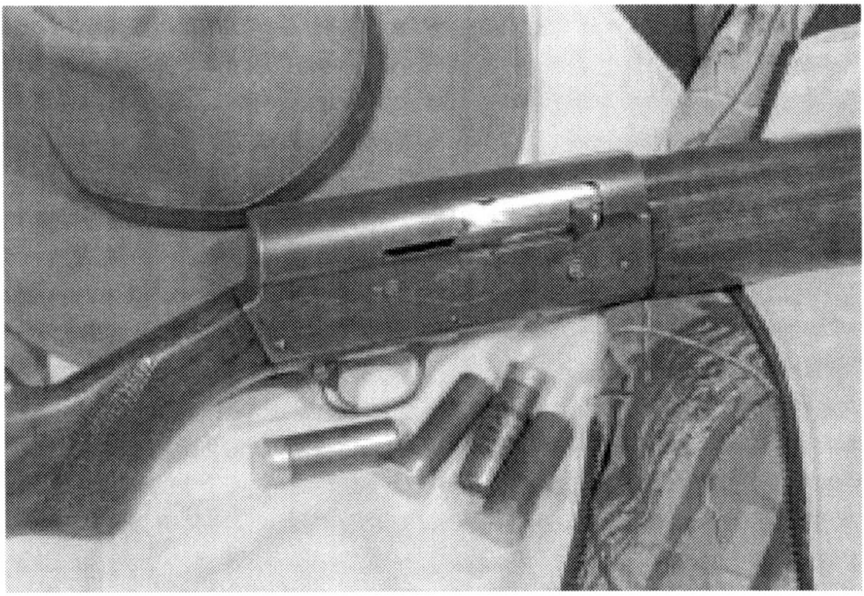

ready for lion and elephant. The hulls were much bigger than the tiny 310 rim fire shells.

But if my father would allow me to use his old shotgun (he never really let me play with his nice Beretta double gun, also a 28 gauge), ammunition was my problem.

Factory ammo prices and availability had not improved any, and, just like my father, I had to resort to reloading or, in my case, hand loading. Most of my father equipment was misplaced or lost when we moved to town, and I didn't have the helpers or the patience to reload the aging paper hulls. So I bought some full brass shotgun shells, primers, shot and gun powder, which could be Elephant FFFg black powder or whatever smokeless powder was available or the lowest price one. Wads were made from old newspaper or even toilette paper, again whatever was handy.

My reloading, or hand loading, gear was as simple as you can imagine. A pocket knife or a big nail to pull out fired primers, a pencil or other piece of wood to sit the over powder wad and a candle to seal the finished shell with some paraffin.

When I started to hunt capivara (*Hydrochaeris hydrochaeris*), or capybara as said in Spanish and English, I became very displeased with the performance of TTT shot, similar to No. 4 buckshot, and the largest shot then available in Brazil, and decided to use slugs. Although we could generally find some cast slugs, IDEAL brand, I saw no reason to pay hard cash for them, and the normal shooting distances inside a swamp or surrounding bush being short as they are; pinpoint accuracy was not really an issue. So, I just fished for some lead sinkers of about the proper diameter in the fishing box and loaded it in my shells instead of shot. The heavier oval sinkers performed much better than the round ones and these bullets stopped more than one capybara with definitive authority.

By the beginning of high school, I finally had a "man's gun" having taken possession of one of my father's 12 gauge trap guns. I was back to a single shot but the 12 gauge was the most powerful firearm that could be legally owned in Brazil. What more could I ask? But, bigger gun or not, the ammunition situation didn't change and I continued with my proven hand loads, just bought new 12 gauge brass shells and looked for larger sinkers.

Not until after I got married did I shoot a couple rounds of trap and some friends allowed me to use their reloading presses to make some proper shells, plastics hulls and wads and 1¹/₈ ounces of 7½ shot. If I remember one thing in particular, it's that those shells kicked much harder than the calves we had in the corral, but I was then a grown man, had a daughter, and had to handle a heavy trap load no matter what. By this time, I was living with my new family in a big city and didn't have much opportunity to hunt or shoot a shotgun and, for several years, I used pistols for much of my shooting; a lot of fun plinking and some less-than-serious competition.

When we relocated to the Netherlands, and I had to leave all my guns behind in Brazil, I desperately looked for some shooting sport. I became member of a pistol club and then a very nice archery club—Frederik Hendrik, in Delft. In the Netherlands, I also shot my first ever round of skeet, in another gun club in The Hague.

When we finally moved to the United States in August 2002, within a week of my arrival in Kalamazoo, Michigan, I was a member of the Southern Michigan Gun Club (SMGC). I found out that its outdoor range was no more than a five minute drive from our new home. Life can be very forgiving at times.

The first thing I did at SMGC was shoot a round of skeet, borrowed gun and shells and, in the next couple weeks, I bought a Remington 870 pump action 12 gauge shotgun and was on my way to shooting several thousand shots a year, mostly in skeet, but some on other clay pigeon games like trap and five-stand and a precious few on upland birds.

If I had a little more common sense and didn't like to collect guns I would not need any shotgun other than the Remington 870. I can shoot it well, it is very, very durable and with the proper barrel it can be used for wing shooting or big game hunting.

But I like to collect guns almost as much as I like to shoot them, and before the end of that year I added a nice 12 gauge Beretta over/under shotgun to my gun safe and in the next year another one, this time in 28 gauge, and I had come full circle.

While the 12 gauge is the most flexible and prevalent shotgun gauge available and it should be the choice for anyone that has only one shotgun (or only one gun), the 28 gauge offers the ultimate in balance between gun size and weight and shot load and if the 12 is the queen of shotguns, the 28 is the princess, slim, beautiful and delicate but with strong enough will to reach out and bring down both pheasant and waterfowl.

My father used a 28 gauge to hunt ducks in Brazil and I used, almost exclusively, my little Beretta 28 for pheasants on the hunt preserve where I train Tupã, my dog.

Another advantaged of the 12 gauge shotgun is that on break-open guns we can use barrel liners or chamber inserts and shoot smaller gauge shells through it, extending its flexibility even more. People will discuss the advantages of one system versus the other, but I believe it is a matter of shooter preference and I used 28 gauge chamber inserts in my Beretta 12 gauge for my first straight round in skeet (25 broken targets in 25 throws).

I also added a very nice Remington 1100 28 gauge semi-automatic to my gun battery aiming at having it as my children skeet gun due to its almost absence of recoil, but if you are a reloader in Michigan, autoloaders and pump guns are, in most cases, a summer proposition, because it is not fun to dig the spent shells from deep, fluffy snow that may cover the skeet fields from December to April, and the little Remington doesn't get all the action it should.

When I finally went on safari in South Africa, I made a stupid mistake and did not take a shotgun along. After collecting all my planned species on the seventh day of a ten day safari, I felt I needed some rest from the serious and sometimes tense pursuit of big game trophy animals.

On a lazy Sunday morning, I borrowed a shotgun and four shells from Ed, one of the professional hunters, and went out for a stroll in shorts and sandals, almost as if I was back to my childhood. I just wandered aimlessly around the property and then Randy and Ed joined me. There were a lot of turtle-neck doves (*Streptopelia turtur*) around but they were extremely difficult to approach and would almost never present the chance for a shot.

Ed asked me to stay behind some bushes and he circled around an open field to flush the birds on the far side hoping some would fly my way. I had one opportunity and brought down one of the fast flying doves with a crossing shot. Unfortunately, I don't have a picture of that dove, but it was as valued a prize as many of the big game animals I hunted.

Just some months ago, I got a new old shotgun that completely changed some of my beliefs in firearms. Jack is a friend that has a small gun shop and takes part in several gun shows in Southern Michigan and one Saturday in Grand Rapids, I met him and we did some trading. I wanted to upgrade my reloading equipment and had a lot of things that did not interest me anymore. We swapped stuff without any cash exchange and when we finished, Jack asked me to see an old shotgun. It was a Savage 720 in 12 gauge, a copy of the famous Browning Auto-5, manufactured in the 1930s. At first sight, the gun looked strange because of the Lyman Cutts compensator at the end of a short barrel, but when I mounted that gun I was sold and couldn't wait for the moment to shoot it.

The day I finally got the gun, there was an open day at the shooting preserve where I train Tupã. I took the old Savage just to annoy George, the owner. George always says that our eyes are side by side in our face, therefore the only gun worth shooting is a side-by-side shotgun and that he would rather miss with a side-by-side than hit something with a "contraption." Because of these kind feelings, I named the recoil-operated ungainly shotgun Georgina. And something else happened, I fell in love with Georgina (and yes, it took me some time to convince my wife that Georgina is a shotgun).

On the two first shots with Georgina, I brought down two birds, a pigeon and a pheasant. The next day at the SMGC skeet field, I scored 22 and 24 out of 25 possible hits. I had to develop a one ounce load to feed Georgina properly but she fits me so perfectly, almost like an embrace, that I would not be troubled even if I had to feed her factory ammo, even if I dislike it.

Happily or unhappily, my love affair with Georgina was strongly challenged after a very short time. After a very sulk day at work I came home in a horrendous mood and told my wife that I was going out to buy something in order to clear my mind. Of course, going out to buy something means going on a gun shop tour, and at the second stop I saw a nice, used double gun misplaced in the new guns rack. I took it in my hands and shouldered the light Spanish 12 gauge and was impressed by its balance and handling. I had the chokes measured and the gunsmith told me that the right barrel was improved cylinder and the left was modified. I just could not resist and brought Laura home (I know, another extensive explanation to my wife).

Because Laura (she was named after the company that made her, Laurona) is very light, recoil with a standard velocity one ounce load is quite sharp, so I developed a low speed $^{7}/_{8}$ ounce load that proved deadly both at the skeet field as well as on upland birds. It is impressive how proper and gentleman-like we feel hunting pheasant over a nice dog with a side-by-side shotgun, even if it is not an English best gun.

Speaking of load development, I came a long way from my hand loading and today use modern progressive presses that spit a finished shell every time I cycle the operating lever and that can produce between two and three hundred shells per hour so I can comfortably shoot my several hundred shots per month and more than a couple thousand per year with relative short time at the reloading bench.

One important aspect I may have failed to mention is that, in general, wherever you may find shotguns, you will much probably find a nicer group of people and develop long lasting relationships and true friendships. Also, although shotguns can be as sexy and exotic as some women, they will age much better and, given proper care, will even look better as time goes by. Georgina is over seventy years old and is as fit as a girl.

This is a brief tale of how I shotguned my way in the last thirty years and I hope I can continue to do so for much longer. I can revive almost every moment just by feeling the sweet fragrance of a fired shotgun shell.

The Corpse-Making Machine

Uncle Bolivar was married to Aunt Marília, a first cousin to my father, and their titles follow the common Brazilian practice of calling all elder relatives and family friends as uncles or aunties.

For a small boy living in a farm, he was somewhat of a myth. First, he lived in Santos, a city by the sea and home of the largest harbor in South America, and the sea is full of mystery and adventure. My father has several stories of fishing with Uncle Bolivar in Santos, but those are his stories and he should write them himself. Second, Uncle Bolivar was a very high ranking official of the São Paulo state police forces; therefore he must have been very, very brave. And third, and probably most important of all, he was an outdoorsman, hunter and fisherman, and he repeatedly came to MY home for adventure.

Uncle Bolivar would come visiting and stay for an imprecise amount of time, days or, more likely, weeks. He drove a green Chevrolet *Veraneio*, a classic SUV of the time and also the most intimidating vehicle of the Public Force, originally painted in orange and black with the skull and crossed pistols emblem at the doors. Every time he arrived he would bring gifts, sometimes strange and exciting things like shrimps and lobsters, and gear equivalent to what president Theodore Roosevelt must have taken in his famed, year-long African safari; guns, ammunition, fishing rods, and real hunting clothes, either green or olive drab, from shoes to hat. I can almost see him walking in or out of some classic African movie like *Mogambo* or one of the several Tarzan that were a staple of my cultural diet.

On a certain occasion during one of his many visits, Uncle Bolivar stayed home alone as we had to go out for some family business and when we came back early night all lights in our home were on and every farm employee and their family members were in or around the house. Some tragedy had happened or was underway.

When my father finally made it in the house, Uncle Bolivar was laying in the bath tub, covered in blood and crying loudly that he was going to die. My father quickly attended him and found a small injury, a bite that punctured an artery in one of his legs that he promptly stanched with a handful of sugar.

After sending the entire audience home, my father started the diligences to find out what had happened, immediately questioning the usual suspect, Uncle Bolivar, and asking him why he was drunk. When Uncle Bolivar tried to argue that he was not drunk, my father produced the evidence. Having only one bottle of Scotch whisky at home, my father had prepared a trap and pencil-marked the liquid level against a wall.

So, the story goes that, being alone, Uncle Bolivar drank some whisky, about four or five inches out of the bottle, and then decided to go fishing. He waded into the water and proceeded to launch the cast net, and during one of the retrieves he was bitten in the leg by a traíra (*Hoplias malabaricus*), a primitive and quite aggressive Brazilian freshwater fish, and the bleeding started. The final outcome you already know.

For as much as Uncle Bolivar enjoyed hunting my father tells that he was a very poor shot, and being a very accomplished wing shooter himself, my father used every possible occasion to tease Uncle Bolivar; particularly, a time he came to the farm with the specific intent of hunting codorna (*Notura maculosa*), a tasteful quail-like bird, because he had promised a wildfowl banquet to his friends of the police force and the Canadian School of Santos.

Uncle Bolivar's pride was a Remington 20 gauge semi-automatic shotgun that he called "my corpse making machine". For Brazilian standards that gun was anti-aircraft artillery as the most common shotguns were either single shots or side-by-sides in 28, 32 or 36 (.410) gauges. My father had two side-by-side 28 gauge, a Rossi hammer gun and a Beretta hammerless. He also had am 8 mm (.310) rim fire single shot from CBC. Both hunters agreed to hunt together but my father insisted that each one would keep their own bags, and that Uncle Bolivar could only take home the birds that he shot. They hunted for several days and my father allowed Uncle Bolivar to take the first shot at every flush and in this fashion he killed eight birds. My father totaled 78.

Uncle Bolivar dutifully dressed and cleaned every single bird and carefully packaged them, clearly marking the two different packs in the freezer. He also was very quiet during the next days. It looked like his promised banquet would not sit many.

On the day of his departure, Uncle Bolivar loaded his gear and, after saying good bye to everyone, he went to the kitchen to get his eight precious birds and finally, my father ended the practical joke. He approached Uncle Bolivar and told him "Bolivar, you are a fool. Take all the birds, they are all yours." And then Uncle Bolivar smiled for the first time in several days.

At another of his visits the targets were ducks or more specifically paturis (*Netta erythrophthalma*). On the first day out the dynamic duo, Uncle Bolivar and my father, went together and although the bag was quite nice I am not sure that Uncle Bolivar enjoyed the competitive shooting because he decided to go alone the next day and spent all the afternoon and most of the night getting ready for his hunt. He skinned every duck from the previous hunt, stuffed them and turned them into decoys, taking the care to even plan the neck and head position of each one.

Uncle Bolivar left very early in the morning taking supplies for a day, including a very complete pack lunch that my mother prepared, and only returned early night with one duck and a somewhat disappointed face. My brother Rodolfo, then a young infant, pointed to the lonely duck and said with one finger up "One tweedy."

There was one species that Uncle Bolivar exceeded in hunting and was generally very successful in bringing home a large bag of what was probably the only predator mammal that inhabited our farm, the house cat (*Felis silvestris catus*). Uncle Bolivar's son, also named Bolivar, had a group of friends that loved to eat cat (according to some experts, cat tastes just like rabbit, and you can't tell them apart once head, paws, and tails are removed) and the dutiful father would do his best in facing the dangerous beasts in order to please his son. Although I can only speculate for I was not allowed to come along to hunt the dangerous predator, I believe that Uncle Bolivar hunted the elusive animals around our employees' homes, and since I do not remember of anyone complaining, I imagine that the damage the cats caused to their poultry far outweighed any affection they had for their stranded pets.

In his arsenal, Uncle Bolivar had one gun that I fancied very much, a 36 (.410) gauge garruchão. A garruchão is generally a single shot, smoothbore, break-open pistol that takes a small gauge shotgun shell. They were quite common in Brazil and were commonly used as a snake or small game gun and could be found either in fishing boxes or as saddle guns. I believe that this nice firearm would be illegal in the United States as it would be considered a sawed-off shotgun.

Uncle Bolivar's garruchão had a nice leather holster with a belt just long enough that I could slip it over my neck and carry the piece with the barrel just missing the ground. Oh, how proud and mighty I felt.

Well, on the day of his departure I just would not let the gun go. I grabbed it and cried and I kept it until his next trip by which time my mother had gently taken it away from me. What a prize it would be to at least handle that gun again.

After Aunt Marília had a stroke, we saw very little of Uncle Bolivar and the last time I remember having him at the farm was around the time we were relocating to town. He came rather quickly to get a boat he had loaned to my father, and he was rather unhappy with the boat's shape; all covered in mud and weeds, it looked more like a duck blind than a boat.

After loading the boat on the trailer and hitching the latter to his Chevy, Uncle Bolivar said that he needed a red flag to be able to legally drive on the road. There was no flag anywhere and there was no way that Uncle Bolivar would not comply with the law. My mother finally broke the stalemate. I had an old red table napkin that I only used and was quite attached to, but that napkin was tied to the end of the boat and turned itself into a warning red flag for the long trip to Santos.

I believe I last met Uncle Bolivar at his daughter's wedding. Marília Isabel married a Brazilian Air Force cadet and there was all the pomp and circumstance due to an officer and gentleman wedding and although my father took me to pay my respects to Uncle Bolivar, I was too overwhelmed and embarrassed to say much, even considering all the time we had spent together.

And then, one day came the news that both Aunt Marília and Uncle Bolivar had died. After her stroke, Uncle Bolivar had built a rehab center in their home and every morning he would first bring Aunt Marília to exercise and then prepare breakfast. That morning as he came back to the exercise room, Uncle Bolivar found Aunt Marília dead and then he had a fulminating heart attack. They were found embraced.

Safari Check List

Even if most of the modern safaris do not require the amount of foot traveling over virgin country as the images we picture from the tales and reports of Frederick C. Selous or John A. Hunter, going on safari was one of the most exhilarating things I've done in my life and a great personal adventure. Just imagine that I had the privilege to go on my first safari when I was 35 years old, the same age as Hemingway was when he first met the green hills of Africa and the same number of years that Francis Macomber enjoyed his short, happy life.

The first and probably most critical step to go on safari is to select an outfitter, or guide service. The initial selection is based on the country and type of animal you want to hunt. As most first-timers will hunt plains game, South Africa is the most popular destination, but Namibia is quickly becoming one as well.

I was very lucky with my choice of Mankazana Safari and the Eastern Cape region of South Africa. Not only did I have a wonderful hunt, I also learned a lot from professional hunter and operations manager, Frans Bussiahn. We spent a lot of time discussing hunting practices and ethics as well of what is generally expected from a package safari.

Frans was very honest and straightforward in mentioning that he could not provide better animals than his neighbor; therefore, he differentiated his operation by the quality of the hunt and the hunter's experience. At Mankazana there is no night hunting, no shooting from motor vehicles, no shooting over bait, no canned animals, and no guaranteed kills. Like most South African game ranches, Mankazana also has fences somewhere but they are not a factor in the hunt. There are thousands and thousands of acres where native and exotic species live, breed, and hide from you.

Even as we were coming back home and met other hunters in Johannesburg airport and discussed our experiences, we encountered hunters whose professional hunters did not abide by the same ethical standards as ours. We heard stories of night hunts with artificial lights and shooting from cars.

Be sure to discuss with your outfitters and professional hunter what you expect from a hunt, ask for references and call them. In the hunting world, English is "*lingua franca*," the common language, and a couple international phone calls are a very minor expense in comparison to the investment in yourself you are making with a safari.

You should also use the opportunity to discuss any limitation or handicap you may have and discuss proper arrangements. I am overweight and under exercised and greatly enjoyed my experience. I also met an eighty years old Spanish gentleman in a wheel chair in the Johannesburg airport that was going on safari!

One thing I did different from both the real life Hemingway and the fictional Macomber is that I did not take my wife along on safari, and I am happy about that. My wife is a wonderful person but, if anything, she is very urban and has very limited appreciation for the outdoors. Once you get to the safari operation, be it a full-facilities camp with electricity, running water, hot showers and a kitchen complete with cook, waiters, etc., or a temporary bush camp with very limited resources, you are there for one thing and one thing only, and the operation is tailored to support you at that one thing, to hunt.

There is not much entertainment outside of hunting in places where the hunt is really good, that is a simple fact of life. My camp even had a pool but the best time to hunt in South Africa is their winter and even in a mild winter, the water will be too cold for swimming and even the most loving wife can get bored after so many days all by herself just seeing her loving husband in the evening and then much probably too tired and thorn-scratched to care for anything but a drink.

So, the message is, if your wife is not hunting, plan taking her to Hawaii or Paris, or better yet, you could stalk red deer in Scotland. Of course if the hunter is a wife, the same message applies to her husband. Don't bring him along unless he hunts.

The principle also applies to children but even if your child enjoys hunting, I would strongly caution you against bringing them on your first safari. Unless you decide for an operation that does most of the shooting from blinds, and I am not particular supportive of that, at least not in Africa, you should expect a reasonable amount of physical activity, long walks over irregular terrain, some climbing and, during a stalk, the eventual crawling. Combine that with eventually missing lunch, several hours without a drink and standing still with your rifle on the shooting sticks from a couple minutes to over an hour waiting for the shot opportunity at a dreamed trophy and you may agree that children are a liability on that first safari.

On your next adventure after you tamed the excitement of being in Africa (as if that was possible) and when you may be willing to sacrifice another hour of stalking or eventually not bagging one particular animal, go ahead and bring your children.

Another delicate matter is that of friends and safari since we may either build a lifelong friendship or destroy one in no more than a couple days. The problem in my view comes from an old human weakness, jealousy. Two animals will never be alike, and between two trophies of the same species, one will be better than the other. If you ever read *Green Hills of Africa* you will remember how much Hemingway suffered because his friend always shot a bigger trophy than him. It can really happen.

I was almost ready to never speak to my friend Randy again when, on the second or third day of our 10-day safari, he bagged three animals and shows back in camp with a kudu, the animals that haunted my dreams and made me go to Africa.

Happily, I was very fortunate and my friendship with Randy was only strengthened in Africa. But, a couple weeks ago when our trophies finally arrived, I was ready to go back to Africa because Randy's Impala is so much bigger than mine, even if some of my trophies, including my Kudu, are bigger than his.

Due to small matters as trophy size, professional hunters are very conservative on allowing hunters to see their friend's trophies. There is nothing worse than a sour camp.

Even worse than quarrels or competition over trophy size is a dispute over potential trophy animals since, in many hunts, the opportunity only appears once. That is the reason why many professional hunters, my good friend Frans included, discourage 2x1 hunts, when a single guide takes two hunters a field. Actually, Frans will only take 2x1 hunts in situations like parent and child or husband and wife (or vice-versa) and you already know my opinion on those.

Don't get me wrong, a good friend is just as much an asset at safari as it is in life, but remember that a friend is much different from a colleague or the occasional acquaintance and, worse yet, not every friend enjoys hunting. But such is life.

Now that we discussed who to invite or not invite to come along on safari, let's talk a little bit about equipment. First and foremost, bring good quality, reliable photographic equipment. A good photo album will help you to enjoy the most important moments of your safari time after time after time. It will also allow you to share your experiences and adventures with your family and friends back home. Pictures, especially digital ones, are cheap, and in case of doubt take an extra one. You can always select the better pictures for the album and discard the bad ones, but once the opportunity has passed, you will not be able to take another picture.

Since I am not much of a photo nut, I advise you to take simple to use cameras, one 35 mm and one digital, along with a healthy supply of batteries, film, spare memory cards, and a case to protect everything. In the case of a digital camera with rechargeable batteries, make sure that your equipment is multi-voltage (110-240 V, 50-60 Hz) since a lot of the places you may hunt, South Africa included, use voltage and current different than the United States.

While cameras are great I don't find much practical use for video recording equipment on safari. You can hunt or record a movie, shoot a gun or shoot a camera, but it is quite difficult to do both at the same time. If someone else is doing the movie, it is another story but for me, it is only additional weight that I don't need to carry, and distraction I don't need to have.

Most hunters on their first safari go after the so-called plains game, but if not a misnomer it is certainly misleading. Rather than plains, the hunter is most likely to encounter a mix of rolling hills and quite broken or hilly terrain. As I found out very early on my safari, traditional African hunting is based on stalking the game and in order to stalk the game, one must first climb to a vantage point, glass the country around and locate the prey.

As I mentioned elsewhere, by the first morning of my safari, I realized that whatever you wish to hunt or shoot in Africa it is up a hill, out there, and not exactly on the same hill you are. I climbed more steep slopes in one morning in Africa than in probably most of my life.

Don't be discouraged; just pack a pair of comfortable hiking shoes that provide plenty of ankle support and light gear. And lightness is a very important attribute of your gear because you will have to bear it from dawn till dusk, walking, hiking, climbing or crawling and if you have ever been in the infantry, you will remember that the morning 10 pound load will weigh a ton by evening.

Next to shoes, the most used piece of equipment are binoculars or field glasses. Bring something on the 10 power range but light enough that you can carry all day long. Also, all the professional hunters used the cross shoulder straps in order to prevent injury to the neck and I see no reason not to follow their lead since they carry binoculars out in the field during one year more than most of us will carry in a lifetime.

My personal optic was a ten dollar Bushnell monocular, I believe a 10X20. Although somewhat limited, I was not handicapped at all because the trackers and professional hunters are more likely to see an animal at half mile with naked eyes than you are, even if using a 50 power gyro-stabilized spotting scope. They know the shapes and colors to look for, you don't.

The one optical gear that I had never used before and that I would absolutely recommend you to take to Africa if every PH already didn't have one is a range finder. While I could never find use for one for my 15 feet capybaras shots in the Brazilian swamps or even in the hundred yard deer shots in Michigan, Africa will offer you the longer shots as a rule. My closest shot was at about 170 yards and my longest was just over three hundred. Range finders take a lot of the guess work out of the equation and greatly improve the chances of a first shot kill.

Since the trackers will most likely carry water and a pack lunch for the group, you should not need a day pack or anything like that. I even recommend you avoid cumbersome knives. Even having a nice collection of custom knives, I only took with me my inseparable Swiss Army knife and a custom-made single-blade friction folder that my father gave me. Make sure that your knife has scissors, tweezers, cork screw and bottle opener. Good beer doesn't have twist caps, South African wine is excellent and the scissors and tweezers are very useful for end of the day surgeries like picking thorns or rounding toenails.

And never, never, volunteer your custom knife to anyone. The wreck you may receive back might make you very upset.

One of the most valuable pieces of equipment I took to Africa was a Princeton Tec IMPACT sport light. This small inexpensive flashlight uses four AA batteries and has LED bulbs for very long operating hours, is completely waterproof, will fit comfortably in a back pocket, and was literally a bright star in the African night. On several occasions, that small flashlight was the only light to guide our group back to the hunting car and we used it to finish skinning my kudu.

Besides my two small knives and flashlight, I also attached to my belt a five round Boyt cartridge carrier which combined with the five rounds in my rifle provided me all the fire power required for several days of hunting. The most I ever shot in a day was four rounds, the first shot almost at first light at bushbuck, one before noon at blesbok and the last two shortly before dusk at kudu. In between each animal, we always got back to the hunting car, so if you believe you need extra ammo carry that in the car, there is no need for you to overload yourself.

As for clothing, the hunter should choose darker rather than light colors. The recommended colors are green, brown and olive drab while light khakis should be avoided. The professional hunters would prefer that you blend with the vegetation rather than with the ground.

Another factor to consider is that temperature may vary a lot during the day, from a frost in the morning to very warm or even hot during noon to cool at evening, not counting the effect of wind. Therefore, it is best to dress in layers; you just don't need the same heavy layers that you use to hunt deer or duck in Michigan. I used green cotton trousers (from J C Penney), good wool socks, a T-shirt and a dark color long-sleeved shirt, and an Orvis wool sweeter. I also carried an old green or olive drab Dutch jacket if the morning was colder.

On top of everything was my old felt hat. It worked as well in Africa as when I used it in the Netherlands as my rain guard. Most everyone else used a baseball hat so that classic hat made me look very distinguished.

Camouflage is not really needed if you follow your professional hunter advice and be quiet, and it may be a liability if you are hunting in public land and it may be totally forbidden in many countries.

Since most safari outfitters will provide you with excellent laundry services, any dirty clothes you left behind in the morning will be washed and ironed when you return at evening. There is no reason to pack excess clothing or carry super-sized luggage.

While all the equipment we discussed so far is of utmost need for you to locate and stalk your intended prey, a bullet will bring it down and transform that animal into a trophy, and in order to precisely place a bullet at the animal you need a good rifle.

I took a .30-06 rifle with me and I can guarantee that it is no coincidence that both real life Ernest Hemingway and his creation Mr. Macomber used bolt action rifles in this same caliber. I figured that, if anything, natural evolution takes time to happen and if Mr. Hemingway used his .30-06 for almost all his hunting in the 1933 and 1954 safaris, including lion and buffalo, why wouldn't this great cartridge perform even better with modern bullets?

My rifle is an out-of-the-box CZ550 American with a single set trigger topped up by a Bushnell Firefly 3-9X40 scope, using CZ's rings. I have a Brazilian friend that owns CZ rifles in most calibers between .22 LR and .458 Winchester Magnum and if Mr. Zocca puts so much confidence on CZ firearms, why not trust them? To complement the package, I added a Browning quick detach leather sling; and you will really appreciate a good sling on your rifle. You will carry it a lot.

I always liked heavy for caliber bullets but could not locate premium 200 or 220 grains .30-06 ammo so I chose the Remington Safari grade with Swift A-frame 180 grains bullets. I couldn't have made a better choice. Before traveling to Africa, the rifle and bullet combination was shooting under 2 inches three shot groups at 200 yards from Randy's bench. After getting there, I was never disappointed.

Of the three professional hunters I had contact with in Africa, Frans and Stuart used .270 Winchester rifles and Ed used a .300 Winchester Magnum. Randy took his Ruger Model 77 also a .300 Winchester Magnum. A South African gun magazine that I bought over there ranked the .270, .308 and .30-06 as the three most popular calibers in that country. In the airport, I saw plenty of guys with .243 and .25-06 rifles but I think they are in the light side, especially for gemsbok, wildebeest and kudu. You don't need a super hotrod new magnum but instead, bring a rifle that you are comfortable with and that you can shoot well. Combine that with a premium bullet and you are good to go.

I took one hundred rounds of ammunition to Africa for a 10-day eight-animal package and I used nineteen. Eight sight-in shots, one clear miss at a springbok at about 250 yards and nine animals that went down on the first shot, and two finishing shots, one at a gemsbok at ten feet and one at my kudu at 200 yards or so.

Based on the above averages, I probably have enough ammo for my next four safaris.

A hunter should not have an unfair advantage over the game but once you located a particular animal under fair chase conditions, you should use all legal resources to make that first shot the only one. That's when rifle and ammunition, scopes, range finder, and marksmanship really come together.

There are two pieces of gear that I did not bring to Africa and that I greatly missed, a soft gun case and a shotgun.

In South Africa, the general rule for transporting rifles in the hunting car is chamber empty, magazine loaded, and the rifle either in a gun rack or with its barrel pointing down. A gun case will add greatly in avoiding possible scratches or dents during driving if the rifle is just put inside the car and will protect it from dust if it's being carried in an open rack. Depending on vehicle speed or wind conditions the African dusty can be as gentle to your rifle as sand blasting, scratching scope lenses, damaging metal finishing and even making your gun jam.

Finally, when you feel that you must rest from the serious and sometimes tense pursuit of big game trophy animals, a shotgun can provide all the relaxation that you need. Most every place you may go in pursuit of big game will also offer ample small game and wing shooting opportunities, and in many cases at no additional charge.

Most, if not all, African countries prohibit semi-automatic firearms, so keep your autoloader at home. Pump-action shotguns are generally acceptable and I borrowed a CZ 12 gauge pump and some 7/8 once shells from Ed to use one morning after I had bagged my kudu to go after doves. But side-by-side and over-under guns are probably your best bet from a legal standpoint.

The 12 gauge is not only the most flexible but also the most widely available shotgun shell anywhere you may go hunting and I would select it unless I would be going on an exclusively wing shooting safari. If you bring a gun other than a 12 gauge call ahead to make sure ammo is available.

A safari is a much more affordable and enjoyable adventure than most people may think and it can be made even more so if you select you outfitter, company and gear carefully. Also, remember that you probably already have over 90% of all the gear that you may need.

So, instead of buying more things you won't use, invest that money on an adventure of a lifetime.

Printed in the United States
66508LVS00002B/1-99

9 781424 147212